Memoirs of a
Dangerous Alien

'Never a dull moment!' *The Independent on Sunday*

'An accessible page turner of unusual quality ... a substantial adventure story, funny and observant' *The Sunday Times*

'Fast-moving and funny' *SHE*

'One of the most exciting children's books I've read in a long time' *Book For Keeps*

'Exciting and racy, an unputdownable read' Mind Boggling Books judges

'Really exciting with lots of twists and surprises ... I simply couldn't put it down and I ended up reading it in one night' Mark Ashton for Lancashire County Library Children's Book of the Year

OTHER BOOKS BY MAGGIE PRINCE

Pulling the Plug on the Universe
Here Comes a Candle to Light You to Bed

Memoirs of a
Dangerous Alien

maggie prince

A Dolphin
Paperback

Published in paperback in 1995
by Orion Children's Books
a division of The Orion Publishing Group Ltd
Orion House
5 Upper St Martin's Lane
London WC2H 9EA

First published in Great Britain in 1994
by Orion Children's Books

This edition published in 1999

A catalogue record for this book
is available from the British Library

Typeset by Deltatype Ltd, Birkenhead, Merseyside
Printed in Great Britain by Clays Ltd, St Ives plc

ISBN 1 85881 073 6

For Chris, Deborah and Daniel Groenwald
with love and thanks

One

You would not think, to look at me, that I was a dangerous alien. As I sit here in bed, starting to write my story in this hard-backed grey notebook from W. H. Smith's, I can hardly believe it myself.

The notebook is large and new. It opens rather stiffly and as I write, it keeps shutting on my hand. I am bending back its spine so that it stays open. I am bending back my own spine to stretch my muscles and try to relax after this day which has been like no other day, ever.

It all began not so long ago when our new neighbours moved in. I knew from the beginning that there was something odd about the girl next door, despite the fact that she looked and behaved like any other twenty-first century teenager. In fact I think this was part of it. Everything about her was too carefully ordinary, as if she had studied being ordinary until she was very good at it. Most people have something odd about them, don't they. I daresay you do. I certainly do, but you'll find that out later. The strangest thing about Fenella

1

was that she seemed to have a worse fear than most of us, of being in any way unusual.

Fenella and her uncle moved into the Old Rectory next door to us one hot, thundery day in spring. It was the day when everyone was saying that the prime minister had gone mad, the day he did a tap-dance in the House of Commons then slapped the leader of the opposition all around the face.

My parents said it was the weather. It was making everyone feel tired. 'Muggy' my Great Aunt Veronica called it. 'Brings out the daft side of folks.'

Tell me something new then, Mum's despairing look seemed to say.

'Now don't you give me that look, Geraldine,' snapped Auntie. 'I'm not stupid. I know it's really electricity in the atmosphere. So what. It still makes folks daft.'

Mum sighed.

We watched the removal men haul furniture, boxes and an impressive computer up the drive and into the grey, ivy-covered house next door.

'They're not short of a bob or two,' muttered Auntie, staring in disapproval at the pristine condition of our new neighbours' possessions. At her feet her ginger cat, Maureen, known to her friends as Moron, gnawed hungrily at the leg of one of our kitchen chairs.

'Come and sit down, Auntie,' cooed my mother, taking Auntie in a shoulder hold that brooked no argument and propelling the cat into the cat basket with her foot. 'They'll see you, standing there at the window.'

They did. As I was turning away from the window myself (we all have to set Auntie a good example) I suddenly found myself confronting a stare that would not have disgraced a laser beam. A dark-haired girl of about my own age stood in next door's drive, looking over the laurel hedge. She was tall and pale and had large eyes, blue I thought. I smiled and winked at her.

This is absolutely not the sort of thing I normally do. I can't think why I did it then. I suppose I was embarrassed at being caught staring. Or maybe it really was the weather. Whatever it was, I still feel very silly now, writing about it.

I suppose I don't really have to tell you this sort of thing, but I will.

Anyway, almost politely, the girl smiled and winked back, then turned and went into the house followed by a massive, neolithic-looking man with jutting eyebrows, a sweeping black hairdo and no detectable forehead.

I went to get on with my homework, feeling shaken. Was it possible that events were taking an interesting turn in our comatose little village?

We live near Stoke Stiley on the edge of the Somerset Levels. I suppose 'comatose' is only partly true. At Stoke Stiley Twenty-First Century School we are actually into pretty advanced computing and technology. The school's computer system has even been featured on national television, and our teacher, Mr Batworthy, is not only a world expert in computing but was, even then, rumoured to be working on something much bigger.

What we did not know at that time was quite how far his fame had spread.

I rang my friend Peter Baxendale. He lives on Blackbarrow Farm and is interested in birdwatching. It is sometimes frustrating trying to drag him away from his tree creepers and lesser spotted woodpeckers.

'Peter, there's a new girl at the Old Rectory.'

'Oh yes? What's she like?'

'Tall, dark, winks at people.'

'I wonder if she likes birdwatching. Is she coming on the school bus?'

'I've no idea. Be at the bus stop early tomorrow and give me moral support.'

'OK. See you, Dominic. There's a yellow wagtail on the barn. Got to go.'

I hung up and went to have dinner in the kitchen. Mum was ladling bolognese sauce on to plates of spaghetti. Auntie and my younger sister, Julia, were already seated at the table. Auntie had taken her false teeth out and put them next to her place mat where they smiled unrelentingly at her. She grinned back at them from time to time.

Mum slapped spoonfuls of bolognese sauce into the cats' dishes too. Her cat, Perkin, leapt on it, snorting into the rising steam, but Maureen the ginger cat was standing with her tail caught in the cat flap, mewing piteously. Julia released her and placed her in front of her food.

Perkin was a great black bagpipe of a cat. His purring continued uninterrupted while he ate, seeming fuelled by uneven, gusty breaths from somewhere round his middle.

'I'll go round later and see our new neighbours,' said Mum. 'Dad took them a tray of tea and biscuits earlier and said they seemed pleasant.'

'Huh.' Auntie shot a dark look in the direction of next door as she sucked spaghetti from her plate. 'All them computers and osmosis clothes driers. What's wrong with counting on yer fingers and drying clothes over the bath?'

Dad came in from the pub.

'Sorry I'm late, dear. I saw a strange sort of glow on next door's roof so I called round in case their chimney was on fire.'

We stared at him in alarm.

'And was it?' asked Mum. Dad shook his head.

'I don't know what it was. It had gone when I came out. Anyway, everything seems all right.' He washed his hands then sat down and started eating. 'Are they foreigners?' he asked after a moment.

Mum shook her head. 'I don't think so. Their name's Brown. Why?'

Dad shrugged. 'Well I may have been mistaken, but I could have sworn I heard them talking in a foreign language as I came up to the front door.'

'Maybe it was computer jargon,' suggested Mum. 'They seem to have some very advanced-looking hardware.'

Auntie cackled. 'More likely Humphrey had too much of the hard stuff at the pub. Eh Humphrey? Eh? Eh?'

5

'Not as much as the prime minister seems to have had,' commented Mum. 'I could hardly believe what I was seeing on the lunchtime news. Did you see it, Humphrey?'

She told Dad about the prime minister's extraordinary behaviour and later we all sat in front of the television news again and watched in astounded disbelief while the chubby little man with the dandelion clock hairdo tap-danced up and down the Lower Chamber of the House of Commons humming Beethoven's Ninth Symphony, before whacking the leader of the opposition rather hard several times on each cheek.

Two

Fenella Brown did go on the school bus. She was standing at the bus stop looking cold and miserable when I arrived there next morning. She was wearing jeans and a massively baggy grey jumper. Her paleness and all the neutral tones gave her the appearance of an old black and white photograph, the sort they used to have early in the twentieth century. She looked unreal.

Peter was there before me too and had already established that she was not at all interested in birdwatching. The overnight thunderstorm had cleared the air and now it was quite cold. Damp leaves dripped in the chilly sunshine and we were glad when the school bus, a cross between a cattle truck and a milk float, arrived.

The three of us claimed senior privilege and sat in a row on the back seat. Fenella told us that she came from Berkhamsted. Her parents were both engineers working on the French end of the Channel Bridge so she was staying with her Uncle Simon. It had been a blow when he insisted on moving to the country, but the chance of a place at the school which had the pioneering computers had softened the blow a little. Nevertheless she was looking extremely nervous.

'I was going to start school after the Easter holidays,' she explained. She had a slightly gruff voice, as though she had laryngitis. 'Then the strain got to me and I thought I'd have this week first and get to know you all.'

We nodded in agreement.

'Starting a new school's awful. Better to get it over with quickly. The first half hour's the worst,' I agreed. I felt sorry for her. I could still remember what it had been like coming up from Junior School, and that had been with all my friends. Fenella was alone. It would be worse for her. I smiled at her. 'You'll be all right. Here, I'll carry your bag.'

The bus stopped and we escorted her down the steps and into the school grounds.

But Fenella's day at school did not start well. She was in the same class and the same physics group as Peter and me and we were studying new theories on time and space. Half way through the lesson Fenella started giggling. Our teacher, Ms Tuttle, slowly turned and stared at her.

'Is something the matter, Fenella?' she asked coolly. 'Have I said something amusing?'

Fenella shook her head, still smiling. 'Oh, I'm sorry Ms Tuttle. 'It's just what you've put on the board. The formula . . . I mean . . . what about the relative defraction part of the time, space and energy formula? It won't work like that.'

Suddenly in the room there was a low-pitched beeping. It lasted only a moment, and as I sat near to Fenella I may have been the only one to have heard it. But Fenella's face suddenly stiffened and her smile faded.

'I'm sorry, Ms Tuttle,' she said quietly. 'Just my little joke. We followed a different syllabus at my last school . . .' She gave a nervous laugh. Ms Tuttle smiled benignly, clearly reassured.

'Well dear, this is the best formula I have to offer you today, but perhaps you can let me know if you have made any earthshaking relativity discoveries by yesterday.'

We all laughed dutifully, relieved for Fenella that the crisis was over. Ms Tuttle, obviously feeling that she had discovered hidden qualities of humour and repartee within herself, was unnaturally affable for the rest of the lesson.

There were no such crises in the computer lesson which followed. Our computer teacher, old, stooped Mr Batworthy, was relaxed and funny. Computer lessons were usually the highlight of the week and today he was in a particularly good mood because he had been on television the night before explaining some of his pioneering work. The interviewer had asked him why, in view of his international expertise, he chose to continue teaching. He said could they think of anything better to do with new knowledge than to pass it on to the next generation?

It became apparent very quickly that Fenella was already expert in computer techniques, though she did make some odd mistakes. I was glad for her that at least this lesson passed without incident.

That night I heard Fenella and her uncle quarrelling. I was in the back garden, emptying the kitchen bin into the dustbin, and their living room window was open. I could just see it over the hedge. Their voices came clearly through the night air, raised and furious. At first I couldn't tell what they were saying, but then Mr Brown's voice bellowed quite distinctly.

'*English*, you stupid girl. Speak *English*. It must become second nature to you, or you will make mistakes. Your blunder this morning was quite bad enough . . .'

'I'm sorry. I've said I'm sorry, haven't I sir? I'll see it doesn't happen again. What more can I say?' Her voice dropped and I had to strain my ears. 'It's just . . . their knowledge has such gaps. I feel we could teach them so much, sir.'

'*Uncle*, you nincompoop! *Uncle*, not *sir*. Are you incapable of learning anything?'

'Uncle then! Uncle uncle uncle! Oh who cares anyway, Uncle. I'm going to bed. I didn't ask to come here.' Fenella sounded close to tears. The voices stopped abruptly and I returned, puzzled and thoughtful, to the house.

The Easter holidays began the following week. The weather brightened and Peter, Fenella and I went birdwatching one day, then on a picnic another. Several times I caught my parents grinning at each other over what they clearly regarded as my growing infatuation. I sometimes wished they would not insist on being so unremittingly understanding.

On the Wednesday my mother and Julia took Fenella with them on a shopping trip to Taunton. In their sexist way they didn't even ask if I wanted to go and I was left to look after Auntie. Peter came over and gazed blissfully at the tiny goldcrests appearing and disappearing in the ivy on our dead elm tree. The radio played the top twenty in a corner of the sunlit terrace, interrupted only by rather a strange news item about the German president who had been found wandering with amnesia in Marks and Spencer's, while over here on an official visit.

'What are they on, these politicians?' wondered Peter out loud.

We brought deckchairs into the garden and I told Peter about the quarrel between Fenella and her uncle which I had overheard the previous week. He lowered his binoculars and squinted at me in the sunshine.

'Weird. Maybe they are foreigners.'

'There is something odd about them, isn't there?' I lay back in my deckchair and put my sunglasses on. A starling swooped low over the garden and Maureen the cat fled, mewing hysterically, her ginger fur standing on end. From his perch on the shed roof Perkin watched and waited, smiling his dark, malevolent smile.

'Mm.' Peter nodded. 'There is, actually. Very odd, now you come to mention it. Have you noticed how they always watch exactly how you're going to do something, before they do it themselves?'

'Maybe it's because we have such impeccable social

11

graces.' I ran a hand languidly through my hair. 'But no, seriously, I have noticed. You're quite right. They talk very carefully too, but throw in slang as if they'd been practising it. Do you know what I mean? And they smile an awful lot. It's almost as if they want to, well, reassure us.'

'Are you sure she called him sir?'

'Well that's what it sounded like.'

'Maybe she said Simon.'

'I don't think so.'

'Perhaps they're spies.'

'Why come here then? There's nothing to spy on here.' I sat up and drank some combine harvester, a drink which included fizzy apple juice and tomato ketchup. Peter looked at me.

'What about the school computers? They were on television and there was all that fuss about them. Mr Batworthy does go to all those international conferences and he uses the computers for government work as well as for teaching, according to Ms Tuttle.'

We stared at each other. 'There's the other work that they say Mr Batworthy is doing as well, whatever that is,' I said quietly. There was a pause. 'On the other hand we may just be getting carried away. Maybe the Browns are simply weird. Particularly Uncle Simon. He really does look like the missing link.'

Peter grinned, then grimaced at the ketchup which had all sunk to the bottom of his drink. 'Yes. Australopithecus walks again.' (Peter was interested in anthropology too.)

'Pithecus? Pithecus?' screeched Auntie who had just

appeared in the garden waving her walking stick. 'What sort of talk is that? Wash your mouths out you dirty boys!'

Peter sniggered hysterically, but the conversation came to an abrupt halt then because Perkin caught the starling in a flurry of feathers and squawking, and Auntie had to rescue it by beating Perkin over the head with her walking stick.

'It's easy to see how her cat got the way it is.' Peter finished his drink and we both rose and went into the house.

Three

The following day Peter had to go to the dentist so I called for Fenella on my own, immune to Mum's slightly anxious leer. Fenella looked pleased to see me and invited me in to try out a new computer game which she had bought. I hadn't seen the game before. It was called Meringue Utang and consisted of an ape trying to steal cakes.

We played it for a while. It was very boring and I felt at a disadvantage because Fenella was remarkably good at it, with lightning reflexes.

She assured me she had been practising, but I had the feeling that she was lying and simply did not wish to appear as clever as she was. I know some clever girls do this in the presence of dimmer boys, out of a sort of pitying politeness, but I had not expected Fenella to, and I did not like the implications that it cast on her view of me.

Half way through the morning she suggested that we should have a cup of coffee and a snack, so we went into the large, dark kitchen of the Old Rectory. It had old-fashioned cupboards and a flagstone floor and there was even an ancient black kitchen range at one end. I could imagine Victorian cooks slaving in here and scullery maids scrubbing the floor. The small, north-facing window let in hardly any sunlight at all.

Fenella started making coffee, and indicated a tall, brown-painted cupboard.

'There are some biscuits in there. Could you get them out, please?'

I tried to open the cupboard door, which had a stiff up-and-down latch. The latch was stuck. I pulled hard upwards with both hands. With my second tug it lifted and the door swung open. As it did so I realised that something had been propped up on the inside of it, something large and heavy. It came at me, with the door, falling top-heavy from high up. In the split second before it hit me I saw red, staring eyes, a pale, greenish face and a mouth open in a soundless shout.

I hit the kitchen table at the same time as the monstrosity did. A chair crashed to the floor and the coffee splashed on to my shirt. Hearing odd sounds emerging from my mouth, I clamped my hands over it and backed to the far side of the kitchen table, my legs almost buckling under me. I was shaking. I could feel myself vibrating like a road drill. I could scarcely force myself to look.

When I did look, what I saw was Fenella. Her face was whiter than ever and her eyes were staring, appalled, at what lay across the kitchen table. It was the body of a man in his thirties, smartly dressed in a grey, pinstriped suit, with immaculate white cuffs showing against the deathly pallor of his clawlike hands.

'Dominic . . .' Fenella moved at last, not towards me but towards the body. I put out my hand to stop her, but something in her expression rooted me to the spot. 'Dominic . . .' Fenella took the body under its arms and dragged at it. 'Dominic dear, I don't actually quite know how I'm going to explain this.' With a colossal heave which showed surprising strength she lifted the body and crammed it back into the cupboard, then shut the door firmly. Speechless with disbelief I recoiled from her.

'Dominic, don't go. We have to talk . . .'

But I was at the kitchen door already. I had known that the Browns were odd, but not that they were murderers. Now all I wanted to do was make my escape and ring the police before I met with the same fate as the man in the cupboard. I felt as though I might be sick or pass out. I started running.

'Dominic! Dominic!' Fenella's voice sounded frantic.

I ducked as I ran down the gravel drive, half expecting a knife or a bullet in my back, or both. My shirt sleeve caught on a branch and ripped as I ran. I skidded through the gate and into the road, then I was in my own drive and my own front door stood open.

In the kitchen, Auntie was taking a chocolate cake from the oven. She looked round guiltily as the middle of it sank like a stone.

'Hello Dominic.' She gave me a furtive grin. 'Just checking your mum's cake. She's always letting things burn . . .'

'Auntie!' I gasped. I could hardly speak as I struggled

16

for breath. My heart felt as though it had already broken a few ribs.

'Auntie . . . where's Mum? Or Dad?'

She frowned at me. 'Out. Nay. Let me see. In. Yer dad's upstairs.'

At that moment he walked into the kitchen.

'Hello Dom. Back for lunch are you?' Then he looked at me more closely. 'What's the matter? Are you all right?'

I shook my head. Then Mum walked in too. Auntie flung the cake back into the oven behind her back and stared avidly. She loved a drama. I leaned back against the fridge and tried to speak.

'Dad . . . Mum . . . I've just been next door . . . and there's a body in the kitchen.'

Well how else can you put it? It isn't the sort of thing you get much practice in announcing. Their expressions of total incredulity told me that I hadn't put it very well though.

'Dominic, is this a joke?' Mum frowned at me with the expression she uses for anything in really bad taste. I shook my head.

'Honestly Mum. We've got to phone the police. I just opened a cupboard and it fell out on top of me. It was . . . really horrible. I could see that Fenella knew all about it too. She didn't even pretend to be surprised. They're murderers. They must be.'

Auntie gave a shriek and fell back against the washing machine.

'Dominic, that's a very serious accusation.' Dad came

up to me and put his hands on my shoulders. 'Now a joke's a joke, but I think this one has gone too far . . .'

'Dad!' I interrupted him, and I think then that the desperation in my voice convinced them.

'You mean an actual body? A dead person?' Mum put in. I nodded. She and Dad glanced at each other and Dad moved towards the kitchen viewphone.

'Perhaps we'd better speak to the Browns first.'

'No Dad! They're not going to admit it, are they? I'm telling you, Fenella wasn't even surprised to see the body. She was just a bit . . . well . . . embarrassed.' I grabbed my father's arm. 'It could be dangerous for us, once Mr Brown knows I've seen the body. We *must* phone the police.'

So we did. Dad spoke to them almost apologetically, and I felt my first stirrings of misgiving about this course of action then, but told myself that really, we had no option.

Four

The police arrived within fifteen minutes, a tall male sergeant and a chubby female constable who was just finishing a jam doughnut. I was profoundly thankful for their tact in not arriving with sirens blaring and lights flashing. Nevertheless, my mother was looking extremely pale and strained by then.

Auntie had locked herself in the loo, and Maureen the cat, sensing the atmosphere of stress, had started ripping up the hall carpet. As the two police officers walked up to our front door I wondered if I could get away with having a quiet nervous breakdown somewhere. Suddenly I understood those people who go to live in caves on top of the Himalayas.

'Come in, officers. Thank you for being so quick. Here's my son Dominic. He'll tell you what he saw.'

The two officers filled the hall with their large, navy-blue presence. The policewoman was blonde with narrow eyes and a sceptical expression. She sucked the last of the sugar from her fingers.

'So you're the young man who found the body,' she boomed in unsuitably cheerful tones, staring at me in a way that made me feel ungainly as well as a liar. 'It isn't rag week at your college is it?'

'He's still at school. He's very upset,' said Mum protectively.

'No.' I glared at the policewoman. My mother shepherded us all into the living room. The whole thing was beginning to seem more and more like a grotesque social occasion. Auntie, sensing tea in the offing, emerged from the loo.

'I'll put the kettle on,' she beamed.

'No, I'll put it on.' Dad made for the kitchen, knowing from past experience that Auntie's tea was strong enough to tarmac motorways. I sat down to confront the police officers' bright smiles. Their smiles had vanished by the time I finished talking.

'Are you quite sure about this, young man?' asked the sergeant, taking out his radio. I nodded.

'It was the most horrible thing I have ever seen.'

'You do understand that if we're to go around accusing members of the public, we have to be quite sure of our facts.'

'Yes.'

'He was in a terrible state when he came home,' put in my mother stiffly.

The sergeant nodded and accepted his cup of tea from Dad. 'Do you feel up to coming back next door with us?' He stared at me. My heart sank. 'Would it be all right with you?' He turned his gaze on my parents. Mum hesitated.

'It would be rather an ordeal for him. How do you feel, Dominic?'

'Oh, it's all right Mum. I'll go.' I stood up and the two police officers stood up too. Filled with foreboding, I followed them to the front door.

The policewoman took my arm in her own friendly, ample one as we walked down the drive. I knew it was because she sensed my terror, but I still felt as though I were under arrest. We turned in at the Old Rectory gate, marching in silence. Desperately I racked my brains for something conversational to say.

'Er . . . do you find many bodies?' I asked at last. They both stared at me, but never answered because at that moment we rounded a bend in the drive and almost fell over Uncle Simon who was bending down clipping the bottom of the hedge. I nearly had a heart attack, but the police officers smoothly assumed expressions of professional calm.

'Mr Brown?' murmured the policewoman soothingly, eyeing the hedge clippers. Uncle Simon's leathery brows vanished into his hairline.

'Yes? What can I do for you, officer?' He sounded astonished, glancing at me with what looked like genuine bewilderment. I started to develop stomach-ache. It felt like a gastric ulcer. There was no sign of Fenella.

'Would you be so kind as to accompany us into your house, sir?' enquired the sergeant.

Uncle Simon frowned.

'What's all this about, officer? Is there something wrong?' He glared at me. 'What's going on? What are you doing here, young Dominic?'

'Now come along, sir. We don't want any trouble, do

we?' The sergeant's voice had more of an edge to it now. With measured paces the older man accompanied the two police officers back to the house.

We arrived in the kitchen and I pointed weakly to the tall cupboard into which Fenella had crammed back my grisly find. The brown door stood closed again now, its horrifying contents concealed. Fenella was still nowhere in sight. Uncle Simon stood by the sink while the policewoman fixed him with a glare which she obviously reserved for homicidal maniacs. Her colleague opened the cupboard door warily.

'I assume we have your permission to look in here, sir?' he enquired over his shoulder to Uncle Simon. He peered inside. Then he flung the door wide open. Apart from groceries, an iron and an ironing board, the cupboard was empty.

Five

I was in disgrace. The police had obtained a search warrant and searched the Browns' house from attic to cellar. They had dug up the garden and excavated the compost heap, leaving it lying all over the lawn. They had interviewed Uncle Simon and Fenella for hours at the police station, and eventually they had come round and been very angry with me.

I stuck to my story, but in the end I almost began to doubt it myself. Fenella had been forbidden to associate with me.

I had not seen Peter since before it happened. I called for him on the Friday and told him the whole story. He said I should watch the yellowhammers through his binoculars and then I'd feel better. Oddly enough, I did.

'They've obviously hidden it,' he said after a while. 'While you were getting the police they must have put it somewhere even the police wouldn't think of looking. There are bound to be secret places in an old house like that, you know, a priest's hole or something. We ought to go there when we know they're out and really search the place ourselves.'

I stared at him, appalled.

'Look, I'm in enough trouble already. I'm just keeping out of their way now. For all I know they may be planning to do me in too, because I saw the body.'

'Mm.' Peter nodded unreassuringly. 'Quite possibly. Well it'll be interesting to hear what Fenella has to say about it all when we go back to school in a fortnight.'

The thought of Fenella made me feel very miserable. I hated her. She had made a fool of me. I had made a fool of myself. The whole episode was so weird and inexplicable that I began to wonder if I was going mad. There *had* been a body. I hadn't been daydreaming or hallucinating or mistaken the ironing board for a body, which was one of my father's more laughable suggestions. The only explanation was, as Peter said, that the corpse had been moved after I saw it.

Fenella herself seemed to have vanished from the face of the earth too. Perhaps she wasn't actually guilty herself, I thought in a weak moment. Perhaps she was just protecting her uncle. Perhaps she was afraid of him. Perhaps she too had now been murdered by her uncle. It was almost with relief, as well as with profound awkwardness, that I met her that Saturday at the village disco. This was a monthly event, subsidised by the school, and was our village's sole claim to an organised social life for teenagers.

Peter Baxendale and I were early. When we entered the village hall together all the small children were still fooling around at the end of the early session, dancing and spilling their crisps on the floor. A few more of our friends were standing about in groups already, talking and waiting for the lights to go down.

Livia (Ms Bunch, our German teacher, in real life) organised the discos. She was a humourless individual with long, ethnic skirts and a face like a yak. You are probably thinking at this point that I should have said a face like a yak's, but you are mistaken. I do mean a yak. A whole yak and nothing but a yak. Today she was wearing a sequinned top above her skirt and sandals, and was talking to some of the senior girls. Among them was Fenella.

Fenella looked paler than ever in the strobe lights, her facing changing from red to green to blue to white. She looked unearthly, foreign, intangible. She wore an expression of bored aloofness. I felt a wave of rage sweep over me as I thought of how she was responsible for all my misery and humiliation, and possibly for a murder as well.

'Come on,' I said to Peter. 'Let's go and talk to the girls.'

He gave a startled bleat but followed me across the hall nevertheless.

'Hello Fenella!' I roared heartily before she could escape. 'Not still at the police station then?'

Everyone stared at me, and Fenella went very red. It was all the more shocking because she had been so white.

'I have to go,' she said quietly to Livia, whose expression of hardworking bonhomie was faltering a little. 'Goodbye.' Fenella glowered at me and strode from the hall.

'*So* sorry,' I cooed savagely. 'Must have upset her. Better go and apologise.' I raced after her.

Outside in the car park, in the dimness of approaching night, my eyes took a few moments to adjust. A car swung through the gates, its headlights dazzling. I stared around me. A pink streak still hung in the sky to the west. The people from the car went into the hall. They were talking about the prime minister's tap-dance. There was no sign of Fenella.

More footsteps approached on the tarmac, but it was only other parents coming to collect their miniravers from the disco. I could see all the way across the car park and down the road. Fenella could not have gone all that way in such a short time, even if she had run. She must be hiding. I shrugged. It was just another example of her bizarre behaviour.

I felt deflated, sad and furious. I also felt more deeply suspicious than ever. The fact that Fenella couldn't face me showed that I wasn't crazy. She *did* have something to hide. There *had* been a corpse. I wasn't mad or stupid, as the police seemed to think. Who was the man in the cupboard? Had no one reported him missing? Where was he now?

My brain surged and suddenly I had to know. I thought of Peter's suggestion that we should search the Browns' house, and I almost went back inside to get him, but by then I was afraid of being slowed down by the voice of caution. I would find the body or I would find Fenella and force her to tell me the truth.

I started to run silently across the tarmac of the car park, not towards the road, but towards the fields at the back. Night was falling now and I was wearing my black jeans and t-shirt. I was almost invisible in the darkness.

Six

I had decided to approach the old rectory from the back. The gravel drive at the front would be too noisy and too exposed. I crossed the field behind the car park, my trainers getting wet in the long grass.

Night smells were all around me, crushed grass, turned earth, the yeasty smell where the cows had grazed. At the bottom of the field were two barns. I cut between them and climbed a stile on to the towpath of the old canal. It was completely dark now and tiny scratchings and rustlings in the hedge seemed to follow me along. Where the canal passed through the water meadow of Peter's farm I turned away and climbed the hill towards the dark outline of the back of my house, and the Old Rectory.

Lights were shining in both houses and I could hear music discordantly mixed, Mozart from the Browns' house and a rock song on Julia's laser player. At a lighted window of my own house I could see the silhouette of my mother reaching up to draw the curtains.

The Old Rectory was bounded by a high red-brick

wall. Patches of rounded moss covered it in places and they felt warm under my hands. Carefully I started to climb. My wet trainers squeaked and slipped but I found footholes and levered myself up on to the wide ledge at the top. This would do as a viewing platform to make sure the way was clear.

I pivoted into position so that I was lying along the top, parallel with the ground, with a good view into the dark garden. The moon came out briefly, then went back behind a cloud. A breeze blew and a twig snapped. I felt cold suddenly. Bushes rustled even after the breeze had gone. Another twig snapped and I lowered my head flat on to the wall. My heartbeats sounded too loud. Someone was down there.

I lay rigid, little florets of lichen brushing my cheek. The wall vibrated with a faint thud. A shuffling movement sounded in the bushes below. Cautiously I lifted my head and tried to see. Someone *was* there. Could it be Fenella also returning this way to avoid me? Or it might be a burglar, or a late-night gardener, or a bat fancier.

But now he was emerging, and he was none of these things. He was a tall man, the set of his shoulders strangely familiar. He stepped delicately round the rhododendrons and avoided the compost heap, now returned to its original state by an apologetic police constable. He was moving towards the back of the garage. It was then that I saw the vehicle. It was small and black, rather like a covered go-kart. In my surprise I leaned too far off the wall, and the crumbling corner of a loose brick fell with a crunch into the leaves below.

At that moment two things happened simultaneously. The man turned round and the moon came out. The pale light shone on his face. With a hollow feeling in my stomach I clung to the wall, afraid suddenly that I really was mad after all.

It was the corpse from the cupboard.

A lot of things happened at once then. A door clicked and an outside light came on. The corpse bent over and crammed himself into the small black vehicle. I crouched on my knees ready to spring from the wall and escape, although my legs felt like rubber and I doubted whether I could stand.

'I'm sorry you didn't enjoy the disco, Fenella,' came Uncle Simon's voice from the back door. 'It's your own fault really for encouraging that dreadful boy.'

'But that's what people *do*, Uncle,' Fenella answered peevishly. They both seemed unaware of the presence of the black vehicle. At that moment it emitted a soft electronic hum and there was the muffled crump of a door closing. Then, to my astonishment, it shot vertically into the air. Just above the house it stopped, showing a faint luminosity against the sky. It hovered for a few seconds, then started to revolve, slowly at first, gradually increasing in speed, until it was scarcely visible. It became a blur, then was gone.

Uncle Simon's voice was loud enough to wake the dead, if they had not been awake already.

'That is the *limit*!' His furious tones reverberated the length and breadth of the garden. 'First they try and get us arrested, then they ignore the official warning they were given and start sneaking around again.'

Fenella's voice sounded alarmed. 'I wonder what they've done this time, Uncle.'

'I wouldn't put anything past them. Let's just hope we may have scared them off in time. We'd better search the garden to be on the safe side. Maybe they've left two corpses behind this time. Get the daylight probe, Fenella.'

'Yes Uncle.'

Fenella turned back to the house and I wondered if I could now slide surreptitiously down the wall and make my escape. I moved one leg which had become numb and stiff. Another fragment of brick fell to the ground, pattering through the leaves as it went. I froze, but it was too late. I could feel Uncle Simon's prehistoric gaze suddenly fixing on my end of the garden. He took a couple of paces towards me.

'Hello?' he called. 'Who's there?' I didn't move. The back door clicked again and Fenella's footsteps returned. I did not dare to move, although my leg now felt like a Sunday joint from the freezer.

'Point it over there,' came Uncle Simon's voice in tones of ominous calm. 'All right. Switch on.'

It was as though the sun had come up. The whole garden was suddenly bathed in clear morning light. An astonished bird began to sing, and I crouched there, foolishly, visible for all to see.

Uncle Simon gave a resigned sigh.

'It's him again. Frankly, Fenella, this is the last straw.'

I tried to jump, but it was no use. For an elderly man Uncle Simon moved remarkably spryly. He was strong too. He hauled me off the top of the wall by one arm and one leg and let me fall unceremoniously to the ground. Fenella came and stood over me, her face expressionless.

'He might have seen what they were doing,' she said to her uncle.

'Mm. We'll have to question him.'

'I'm sorry. I can explain,' I gabbled, struggling to my feet and hating myself for behaving apologetically. I had been so angry with them and now I was grovelling. But there was something in their eyes, a detached, dispassionate summing-up of me, which was truly frightening.

This, however, was nowhere near as frightening as the gun which Fenella produced from her pocket. I stared at it for a long moment, hypnotised. With a belated, kindly smile she put it to my forehead and pulled the trigger.

Seven

Having expected to be dead, I was amazed, relieved, and degradingly grateful to find that I was merely paralysed. The gratitude didn't last long though. The paralysis was a terrifying sensation. It was like being just a brain attached to a lump of meat, the whole of my body reduced to the same state as my numb leg. I remained standing where I was like a robot with a flat battery.

'You only gave him a two-shot, I hope,' smiled Uncle Simon cheerfully. Fenella laughed.

'No point if he can't speak.' She fetched the wheelbarrow from next to the compost heap and tossed me into it. Like her uncle, she seemed to have astonishing strength.

I felt no pain as the barrow jogged and bumped over the uneven ground. The two Browns talked across me as though I were, in fact, compost.

'He's seen too much now, hasn't he Uncle?'

Uncle Simon inclined his head.

'It'll have to be the brain processor. No alternative.'

Brain processor? They must be spies, and yet . . . My mind fought to cope with the possibilities. I had read as much science fiction as anyone else, and was pretty keenly tuned to expect alien life forms invading us at any moment. But this was real life, not a story where anything could happen.

'It'll take a day to Ismos and back. How will he explain his absence?'

Fenella turned and backed up the two steps into the kitchen, pulling the wheelbarrow after her. Her uncle helped her steer it across the kitchen and into the warm, beautifully furnished living room.

'Oh, no problem. The Starship Dupronic is docked at the Alpha Centauri Interchange, with brain processors on board. We'll have him there and back before the disco finishes. Right Fenella, you find out what he knows while I go and put the kettle on.'

At this point I was suffering from total suspension of belief. Quite kindly, Fenella lifted me on to the sofa and arranged a cushion behind my head. She smiled at me and sat down on a velvet-covered footstool, facing me.

'Poor Dominic, I'm afraid this must seem very odd to you. Never mind, we're soon going to wipe it all out of your head and you'll just think you had a lovely time at the disco. But first I want you to tell me what you saw in the garden. Did you see anyone trespassing, besides yourself?'

I tried to nod but my head was rigid.

'Yes,' I croaked.

'And who was it?'

Despite my rigidity I still managed a profound shudder.

'It was the corpse,' I whispered.

'Yes.' Fenella grimaced apologetically. 'Sorry about that. Was there just him, or anyone else?'

'Just him. It was more than enough.'

Briefly something flashed in her eyes, as though a different person lurked behind them, then she went on with her questioning.

'And what was the corpse doing?'

'I don't know. I couldn't see.'

Uncle Simon re-entered the room and cut in brusquely.

'Come on now, lad. You must know. You were there, spying. What did you see?'

'I only realised he was there just before you found me,' I protested weakly. 'I don't understand all this. Please tell me what's going on. What are you going to do to me? Where do you come from?'

Uncle Simon glared and tapped his foot on the soundless carpet.

'These Earth fools can't even spy properly. All right Fenella, get him ready for transportation. You can take him up yourself. I've had enough of pin-brained aliens for one night.'

'Oh, thanks Uncle. Can I be language-processed for German while I'm up there, please? There's a school trip to Munich in June.'

Uncle Simon frowned. 'More gallivanting? You'd better ask at Central Control. Off you go now.'

By now my sense of reality had slipped seriously. Either I was dreaming, or I was mad, or they were mad, or . . . surely not . . . they were from outer space . . .?

Several things were clear though. I was their prisoner,

I was in danger and I was about to have something unspeakable done to my brain. I felt a creeping horror, a greater fright than I had ever experienced.

As Fenella lifted me back into the wheelbarrow I tried to cling on to the heavy maroon velvet of the sofa. I tried to grab at the long tapestry curtains with little shepherdesses on them as she wheeled me out of the room. I tried to wake up. One does feel paralysed in dreams, I told myself. This had to be a dream. But the nightmare continued.

'OK,' said Fenella as we arrived in the garden. 'I'll have to release your legs to fit you into my gravity-blaster. If you try to get away I'll have to incapacitate you again.' She pointed her gun at my legs and as a green light glowed in the barrel, feeling returned to them.

I ran. I stumbled and blundered towards my house where lights shone and Mum, Dad, Julia and Auntie would be watching television. At once my legs became stiff and numb again and I toppled, like a shop dummy, into the potato patch. Fenella sighed.

'You won't need brain-processing if you keep on hitting your head like that.' She slung me over her shoulder and set off towards the garden shed.

'Fenella, what's going to happen to me? I don't need brain-processing, whatever that is. Please put me down.'

'I'll tell you about it as we go,' Fenella replied, steadying herself as she opened the shed door with one hand, the other still gripping the backs of my knees. 'Bye Uncle,' she called behind her.

Inside the garden shed stood two more vehicles similar to the one in which the corpse had flown away. The first of these was bright red and more streamlined than the corpse's.

'Lovely isn't it?' Fenella beamed at it and lowered me very awkwardly into one of the two seats. 'It's this year's model. Now Dominic, I don't want you to be afraid. I know you are, but there's no need.' She slid into the seat beside me. I looked at her.

'Fenella, please let me go.'

She glanced away. 'I can't.' She pulled a seatbelt across me and clipped it into place, then she did the same for herself. A glass dome closed over our heads.

'You could, you know.'

I wondered if I had imagined her brief moment of weakness. She shook her head firmly now.

'No, I can't. We're not going to hurt you, Dom. We're actually here to help you, Uncle Simon and I.' She seemed to be avoiding my eyes. 'We are here to help your whole planet. I suppose there's no harm in your knowing, since it will soon all be wiped out anyway.' She glanced up and so did I. Above our heads two flaps were opening slowly in the shed roof.

'Fenella, I can tell you don't want to do this. We were friends, remember?'

She compressed her lips. 'Don't try emotional arm-twisting on me, Dominic. Some things are more important than friendship. You must be aware of how your international affairs here on Earth have deteriorated since the Russian Civil War. You're teetering on the brink of all-out international conflict again, after all those years of relative peace. You're not stupid. You've obviously realised that we're from outside your planet.'

The shed roof was open to the sky. Fenella touched a button and a low vibrating hum began in our small vehicle. I found I was gritting my teeth in terror.

'You've discovered too much about us, Dom. I'm sorry. It's partly due to our carelessness and also partly because of some interfering busybodies from another planet who don't know any better, poor souls, than to fall out of cupboards pretending to be corpses.'

She flicked her fingers over the wide control panel, moving with lightning touches. I was reminded of the computer game. With breathtaking speed the vehicle shot into the sky. I must have gasped aloud because Fenella glanced at me.

'I'm sorry.'

The gravity-blaster began to rotate clockwise, increasing relentlessly in speed while a high-pitched whine built up in my head. I could no longer hear what Fenella was saying. Streaks of darkness blurred my vision, then darkness itself.

Eight

When I regained consciousness I felt violently sick. I looked around for a bucket, which needless to say your average flying saucer does not carry. Fenella turned from the controls and touched my forehead.

'Lean your head back. I'll give you a travel sickness tablet.' She rummaged in the canvas bag she took to school with her and produced a packet of Joyrides. 'I'd forgotten how sick hypervortex travel makes you the first few times.'

I took the tablet and lay back in my seat until the sickness receded. I realised that my paralysis had gone too. I flexed my limbs cautiously. They felt quite normal again. Carefully, fearing some new physical catastrophe, I pulled myself upright in my seat and looked around me.

We were in space. All that separated us from the vast hollowness of the universe was a thin glass dome. There was emptiness above and below our tiny craft. If it had not been for the gravity-blaster's astonishing forward momentum of speed, I felt we could have dropped for ever into the void.

The stars were amazing, massive and glowing. I had never seen or imagined them like this. They were like Piccadilly Circus plastered all over the sky. I felt a ridiculous desire to burst into tears.

'Cup of tea?' enquired Fenella. 'I'm on automatic control for a while so we can relax.' She pressed a button and a paper cup dropped down into an alcove in the wall and filled up with tea. 'Milk and sugar?' She handed me the steaming cup. I recoiled from it suspiciously. 'It's all right, Dominic. It's just normal tea, and the artificial gravity's switched on, so it won't float out of the cup.'

'Thank you.' I accepted the drink, still apprehensive. Fenella sat back and regarded me, sipping her own cup of hot tea very slowly.

'So what do you think of my gravity-blaster? It does one point five parsecs per hour.'

I looked at her with incredulity. 'Well that's dreadfully impressive, Fenella, but I can't think of anything I wanted to know less.'

She sighed. 'I suppose you're being quite reasonable under the circumstances.'

'And will I still be quite reasonable when you've detached my brain, or whatever it is you intend to do?'

'Oh, amazingly reasonable . . .' She cut herself short as if she had been about to say something quite different. 'Dominic, all we're going to do is remove from your memory any parts which are an inconvenience to us. And perhaps lessen your curiosity a little. It's quite painless. We've already had to do it to several people from different parts of Earth . . .'

'You mean there are more of you aliens down there?'

Fenella paused. 'Oh yes. A lot of us. We had to come, you see. This new international confrontation on Earth ... well it's just too serious. It's these new fusion bombs you've started producing, and ... something else too. The point is, you're threatening the entire galaxy.'

She stared ahead into the white blaze of stars.

'And the something else?' I spoke very quietly. 'Surely you can tell me, if you're going to erase my mind.'

Fenella paused again and ran her fingers along the top of a small computer screen. I could hardly hear her when she spoke.

'You've discovered the hypo-relativity syndrome.' Her eyes flicked sideways at me. 'You've discovered how to travel faster than light.'

I tried not to gape at her. 'Go on.'

'You now have the means of sending people into outer space, not just ambling around your own little solar system the way you have been doing. Two scientists, one in Britain and one in America, have discovered it at more or less the same time. It makes interstellar travel possible in quite manageable periods of time. Just imagine how we feel at the prospect of having you lot blundering about out here with your bombs and your raving paranoia. We actually have a nice peaceful universe most of the time.'

'Well you would have, wouldn't you, if you plug people's brains in whenever they get out of line.'

She really stared at me then. I went on, wanting to upset her poise, wanting to make her angry with me.

'So you have a nice peaceful universe most of the time. What about the rest of the time?'

'Oh.' She shrugged. 'There are always a few lunatics about. The worst are the Black Star Gang. They go around gibbering about human rights . . .'

The small computer screen flickered and crackled. Fenella touched a button.

'Dupronic? Come in Dupronic?'

There was no reply. I stared ahead. We were flying in the direction of a particularly dazzling star.

'Is that where we're going?' I asked.

Fenella nodded. 'Yes. That's Alpha Centauri. At least that's what you call it. We have an outpost space station orbiting it, the Alpha Centauri Interchange, where our Starship Dupronic is docked at the moment. It's the last point of civilisation in the populated galaxy before we get to planets like yours.'

She had obviously decided to go on the offensive again. I stared at her coolly.

'We may not be as advanced as you are, but we certainly don't drag people off into space and interfere with their brains.'

Fenella laughed and turned back to the controls.

'But you would if you could. Dupronic? Come in Dupronic? This is Gravity-blaster Nightwatch.' A button glowed but there was still no reply.

I suddenly realised that there were a lot of questions I wanted to ask Fenella before my brain and I parted company.

'What do you mean when you say "we"?' I asked her after a few moments.

'I mean the United Council of Planets. I'm employed by them on a work experience project as a watcher on your planet.'

'What are you going to do to our planet? Why come to Somerset of all places?'

'Somerset? Oh, didn't I say? The British scientist I mentioned – you know, the one who discovered the hypo-relativity syndrome – well it's Silas Batworthy. Don't look so astounded, Dominic. He's one of this century's greatest geniuses and we have to stop him. He could be quite useful to us on computers, though, if we brain-process him carefully. As far as Earth's concerned, well there are various things we might do. We've had aggressive planets before. One of them we blanketed with peace gas, a sort of tranquilliser. On another one, a very small planet, we brain-processed every single person there. That was terribly expensive though and I don't think the Council would do it again.'

I felt weak with horror.

'You're barbaric. Don't you think people have the right to work out their own solutions?'

'More tea?'

I held out my cup. 'I just can't believe it about Mr Batworthy. I mean, I can believe he's a genius, but I can't believe you're contemplating destroying his brain.' I shook my head and stared at Fenella as she handed me the refilled cup.

'You're an alien, an actual alien, and I'm sitting here looking at you,' I whispered.

Fenella laughed.

'No Dom, *you're* the alien, the very dangerous alien actually. *I'm* the normal human being.'

As she spoke, a buzzer sounded on the control panel. She pressed a button and spoke in a strange language. It sounded like Anglo-Saxon spoken by a mad parrot. The small screen glowed and a voice spoke in English.

'This is the Dupronic. Hello Gravity-blaster Nightwatch. Hi Fenella. How are things?'

'Hi Mitzalie. Fine thanks. I'm bringing up a candidate for brain-processing. I'll program the computer myself when I get there. There's something wrong with my screen. I can't seem to get a picture.'

'I think it's interference from the Dupronic's invisibility screen. It should clear shortly.' The voice sounded unplaceably familiar. It went on. 'Uncle Simon called to say he's following you up with another candidate for brain-processing.'

Fenella rolled her eyes. 'Oh dear. He won't like that. He was going to settle down and watch the late night horror film on television.'

Suddenly the screen cleared and a face appeared on it. I gripped the sides of my seat.

'Hi Dominic. Found any good bodies lately?' enquired the face. I had to look twice before I could believe what I saw. It was the young policewoman, this time minus her doughnut.

'Oh no . . .' Words failed me. Fenella smiled as she operated the controls.

'Of course, you've met Mitzalie, one of our senior watchers, haven't you.'

I closed my eyes. If even the police had been infiltrated by aliens, what hope was there left for any of us?

Nine

The Starship Dupronic was a breathtaking sight. It was a shining, black, flattened cone. Lights shone from windows around it. Beyond it the Alpha Centauri Interchange hung like a floating city in space, with lighted domes and covered streets just visible. In the streets I thought I could see trees full of leaves and blossom, and the tiny figures of people moving to and fro. For a moment I wondered if anyone there could help me, then I realised what an absurd hope that was. All those people must obviously be employed by the United Council of Planets.

At least I knew now why the police had failed to find any trace of the 'corpse' I had seen. I wondered which other seemingly normal human beings were in fact aliens. Who was there left to trust?

Fenella was operating the controls as we drew near to the Dupronic.

'Gravity-blaster Nightwatch approaching the Rogery Inlet. Do I have clearance to dock?'

Why was she speaking English?

'Clearance granted.' Ahead of us a flap slid open in the gleaming black hull. Fenella looked at me.

'Dominic, do I have to put you out of action again or are you going to be good? There isn't actually anywhere you could run to.'

'Why were you speaking English just now?'

'Oh . . .' Fenella shook her head. 'We all have to practise our English while we're on this project, technical staff on the Dupronic, everybody. It's for practice, so that any of us who have to go down there will sound completely convincing. Now what about this?' She waved her gun at me. I wondered about taking it from her, then realised what a waste of time that would be without any means of getting back home again. I felt so weak with fear, anyway, that it was almost like being paralysed again. I shrugged.

'No. Don't bother. I'll be good.' It seemed that there was nothing I could do now to prevent my brain from being tampered with.

We docked in a small hangar where there were spaces for three more gravity-blasters. Fenella slid back the glass dome and helped me to my feet.

'How do you feel?'

'Wobbly.'

As I spoke a tall woman in what looked like red pyjamas came striding into the hangar.

'Ah, Fenella, now what's been going on here?'

I tried not to stare at her but it was difficult. For one thing her hair was red. I mean really red, crimson, like tomato ketchup. For another her eyes were extremely widely spaced, like a sheep's, so that whilst one eye looked at me, the other seemed to be inspecting her left ear. I experienced a new surge of incredulity, the sort of unreal feeling you get with a very high temperature.

'Parry, this is Dominic Gaunt. Dominic, this is Parry who runs the work experience project.'

I shook hands nervously, half expecting to be electrocuted by so much redness. I wondered at the same time if hand-shaking was genuinely a social habit up here or whether she was just doing it to make me feel at home. Parry looked bored.

'Leave the space doors open, Fenella,' she said in a strangely over-emphatic voice, as though she were speaking to an idiot, when Fenella moved to press a button. 'Simon will be here at any moment with someone else for memory erasure. It seems you were seen taking off in your gravity-blaster. You really must be more careful. There are plenty of other people who would like to go on this work experience project, you know.'

Fenella flushed.

'I'm sorry, Parry.'

'I'm afraid I'll have to refuse your request for language-processing in German because of that piece of carelessness.'

I looked at Fenella to see how she was taking this. Her expression was unreadable. Parry strode down the hangar to the space doors.

'I gather you've had some trouble with the Myrions, Fenella. You'd better tell me about it while we wait for Simon.'

Fenella sighed.

'They seem to be trying to sabotage the project, Parry. I think their aim is to discredit the watchers. I suppose they think if they make things awkward enough for us we'll have to keep leaving and being replaced by other people and the whole enterprise will become too inconvenient and expensive. One of them hid in a cupboard and pretended to be a corpse. He fell out on top of Dominic.' She smiled at me suddenly in an unnervingly human way. 'The planet Myria doesn't agree with our . . . er . . . help for your planet.'

Parry frowned and shook her head sadly. I could see that she was an expert in the more-in-sorrow-than-in-anger technique. She clicked her tongue and sighed.

'Despicable. What with them and the Black Star Gang, I don't know what the universe is coming to. Personally I think the Black Star Gang is behind it all. They'll stop at nothing to try and prevent the spread of civilisation. Once we manage to get that lot through the computers I think the Myrions will give up too.' She turned to me. 'Poor Dominic. This must all have been very upsetting for you. Never mind. You can be quite certain that up here we will only do what is best for you. We are here to help you.' She smiled at me. It was an unsettling experience. I looked away into space.

It suddenly occurred to me, looking out through the space doors in an effort to avoid Parry's two-pronged gaze, that I was standing with nothing between me and space and not suffocating. As if reading my thoughts Fenella nodded towards a control box on the far wall.

'Artificial air and gravity. We switch it on all round the ship while she's docked.'

Parry clicked her tongue again.

'Fenella, this is not a guided tour. The sooner you get this lad brain-processed and back to Earth the better.'

As she spoke a bronze-coloured gravity-blaster blazed into sight, reflecting the light of the great star behind us. It hurtled towards us, then slowed effortlessly as it passed through the hangar doors.

'Oh good. Here's Simon now.' Parry stepped forward as it stopped and the glass dome slid back. The bad-tempered face of Uncle Simon appeared. He rose to his feet and I peered round him to see my fellow victim, almost glad at the prospect of being joined by someone else from Earth, but sorry that another human being should suffer the same fate as me.

A thin figure was inside the tiny spaceship. He looked sick and miserable. It was Peter Baxendale.

Ten

'Fenella, we wouldn't tell anyone. Who would believe us anyway?'

'It's no good,' I muttered to Peter. 'I've tried all that. They won't listen.'

We had to walk quickly to keep up with our captor as she strode along the corridors of the Starship Dupronic. Behind us marched Mitzalie, the plump policewoman, her gun aimed at the backs of our heads. Fenella ignored Peter's remarks.

'How did they catch you?' I spoke to him in an undertone.

'I followed you. I saw Fenella drag you off into the garden shed and then the flying saucer leave, but before I could go for help, Uncle Simon discovered me.'

'Get a move on,' said Mitzalie sharply. 'Stop mumbling.'

I looked at her with loathing and we marched on.

Fenella, Peter and I looked very much out of place in our Earth clothes. Everyone else, including Mitzalie, wore versions of the loose-fitting trousers and tops which I had seen on Parry. The presence of so many pairs of pyjamas only added to my sense of being asleep and dreaming.

The long, straight corridors were lit by small lamps, high up, which shone with what looked like daylight. Glass doors through to offices, recreation rooms, store cupboards, laboratories and computer rooms punctuated the walls. At intervals there were large windows out on to space. The floor was carpeted with a sort of bouncy beige towelling which was remarkably easy to walk on. An atmosphere of businesslike normality prevailed everywhere. I could have believed that I was in any busy office block or scientific establishment if it had not been for the views of space, and the people.

At first glance they looked human enough, but bit by bit I realised that some were abnormally tall or short and some had strange colouring. Bluish or greenish hair was quite commonplace, like crowds of daring grannies. A few looked like Parry with wide-set eyes and several obviously came from the same planet as Uncle Simon because they also had somewhat prehistoric features. One woman, lurking in a corner, had a greenish pallor similar to that of the corpse in the cupboard. I noticed that Fenella and Mitzalie gave her an unfriendly stare.

Fenella acknowledged several other people as we walked, and Peter and I received a number of curious glances. Mitzalie stopped to talk to a small group of people who were standing in the corridor eating sandwiches, or at least layered strips of food of some kind. I wondered about making a run for it and I tried to catch Peter's eye. I wondered if there might be any help to be had from such people as the Myrions or the Black Star Gang, if one could find them.

'. . . awful trouble with the Myrions,' Mitzalie was saying. It was bizarre that these aliens all spoke English. I wondered desperately if this was, after all, really some complicated and sophisticated joke?

'Oh, those Myrions, they're such a pain. The Council are thinking of banning them from interstellar missions.' The speaker, a young man of about Mitzalie's age, glanced over his shoulder guiltily, like anyone anywhere making a racist remark. 'You never know if even the processed ones are really trustworthy.'

'Thank goodness they have so few representatives on the Council now . . .'

We all moved on. I don't know whether Fenella had seen the slight movement of my head towards Peter, but she grasped my arm firmly now.

'Would either of you like any new languages while you're up here?' she enquired. 'You might as well feel that something good has come out of this. It's a simple matter for the computers to implant new languages into people's brains.'

Peter looked interested suddenly. 'I wouldn't mind French and German . . .' His voice trailed away as he saw my expression.

'If you're going to forget everything you won't know why you're suddenly so good at them, will you?' I snarled. 'And it wouldn't do for us to start thinking inconvenient thoughts, would it?'

Peter looked as though he thought I was making a

mistake in antagonising the enemy. He shrugged awk-wardly at Fenella.

'What do your spaceships run on?' he asked, changing the subject. Fenella smiled at him approvingly.

'Cosmic radiation,' she replied. 'It's everywhere up here so everything runs off it, even our tooth-brushes.' She laughed lightly, flashing her perfect teeth, then stopped in front of some lift doors and pressed a button. We waited in silence for a few moments, the four of us so close together that I could feel Mitzalie's gun digging into my shoulder.

'This Black Star Gang, what do they do exactly?' I asked. Mitzalie and Fenella glanced at each other.

'They have the ridiculous and subversive idea that everyone should stop being brain-processed,' Mitzalie replied, 'and they help planets which want to opt out of the system.' There was a strange angry glitter in her eye. 'They have no respect for authority.'

The lift arrived and we moved towards it.

'Hang on.' I held back. 'What do you mean, *everyone* should stop being brain-processed?'

Mitzalie waved her gun. 'Get in. I don't know why you're looking so surprised, Dominic. Of course we're all brain-processed by the computers. It's for our own good. It wipes out selfishness, bad memories, night-mares, aggression . . .'

'It docsn't seem to have worked on you,' muttered Peter. I threw him an astonished but pleased glance, then turned back to Mitzalie.

'You mean . . . let's get this clear . . . everyone up here is brainwashed?'

Mitzalie sighed as we all entered the lift and the doors closed behind us. 'No Dominic. Everyone is helped. Brain-*processed*. We're all made into much better people by our monthly session with the computers. We all feel much happier for it. What you are expressing is simply an unreasonable prejudice.'

The lift stopped and the doors opened. Even more endless corridor confronted us. We stepped out but then I stood completely still. Peter stood by my side.

'Can't you see how wrong it is?' I asked the two girls. 'You're keeping people in line by depriving them of reality. Where is the value in having a universe full of zombies?' They both laughed and shook their heads in a patronising way, and escorted us across the corridor to two glass doors which had strange writing on them. The doors slid open at our approach just as though it were Sainsbury's. Then even Peter's pragmatism suffered a blow. The entire far wall was dominated by a massive computer, and protruding from the bottom of it was a row of coffins.

They were in fact body-sized drawers. There were about forty of them. Some were closed and some stood open. The computer was clicking and humming and various coloured lights winked on and off. A man in white pyjamas was sitting at one of a number of keyboards.

'Hi Marky,' called Fenella. 'I'll program these two. They need specific erasure.'

Peter and I backed in unison towards the door. Fenella sighed and produced a gun from her pocket.

Mitzalie closed in behind us. Parry appeared through another glass door at the side.

'Don't be afraid,' the red-haired multi-gazed alien snapped. 'It really won't hurt at all. Now please each get into one of these capsules.' She gestured towards the coffins and our two captors raised their guns and pointed them at our heads.

'I won't do it,' I said. Peter stood wordlessly next to me.

'Look, I really don't want the watchers to have to incapacitate you both again. Too much of it can be extremely bad for your nervous system.'

'This is *all* extremely bad for my nervous system,' Peter muttered.

'Go on,' urged Fenella. 'You won't feel any different afterwards. You won't even know this happened. We'll just push the drawers into the computer, then you will feel a sort of clamp come down on your head. Then you'll go to sleep. When you wake up you will be back in your own beds. Now please get into the capsules.' At a sign from Parry she and Mitzalie pressed their weapons to the sides of our heads. We got into the capsules.

Inside, the capsule was high-sided, horrific. It was lined with padded plastic or something similar, material to absorb sound. I wondered what they did about people with claustrophobia. Programmed it out of them, I suppose. I stifled terror and tried to loosen my clenched hands and gritted teeth. I could no longer see Peter.

'Dominic?' I could hear him calling.

The alien faces loomed above me, Fenella and Parry, smiling, smiling, smiling.

Parry moved away. 'I'll leave you to it then, girls.' The tap of her footsteps receded across the room. Fenella moved round to my feet.

'Don't worry,' she said suddenly, and winked, as she had done the first day I saw her. Then with a smooth push of her foot she sent the drawer sliding backwards into the depths of the computer, and me head first into total darkness. The last crack of light vanished as the drawer stopped with a bone-shaking thud.

I lay very still. It was like being buried. There was room to move about in the drawer but I didn't dare to, for fear of what I might touch. I fought against suffocating feelings of panic and waited for the clamp to come. In a frenzy I thought through the events of the past few weeks, trying to impose them irreversibly on my brain. The corpse, the gravity-blasters, the flight into space. Remember, remember. Slowly I felt myself drifting into sleep, and still the clamp had not come. I fought for consciousness, knowing that I was losing the battle. A force stronger than I was had decreed that I should sleep, and sleep I must. My last thought as I passed out was that still, the clamp had not come.

Eleven

There was bumping in my sleep, and nausea. The bedclothes were too hot and I was glad to wake up. Was it a school day or a weekend? No. No, of course, a holiday. It was the Easter holidays. But I must be ill. I felt strange. Surely I wasn't going to be ill for Easter.

I opened one eye and looked at the curtains. Light stabbed brightly in through a crack between them. I could hear sounds as though I had been drugged. Had someone spiked my drink at the disco?

The dreams ... how odd the dreams had been last night. I struggled to remember them, knowing how quickly dreams can be irretrievably lost once you wake. But these dreams were not lost. They were not lost at all. Quite the reverse in fact. They were becoming clearer every minute.

I pulled myself up against the pillows and half-sat, half-lay, staring at the wall. My sickness receded and my headache faded away. A deep astonishment filled me and I realised that this was the day I had not expected to experience with a whole mind. Yet I was doing so, or so it seemed. How could one tell? Where, after all, was the line between reality and unreality? I felt as though I could remember everything, all of last night's terrifying events down to the minutest horrifying detail.

I tried to understand. Could it be that the computer had malfunctioned? Cautiously I swung my legs out of bed. I felt a bit dizzy but nothing worse than that now. I stared around me. Everything in my room looked normal and familiar. My Rupert Bear wallpaper (an indication of the frequency with which our house is decorated) curled off the walls in the corners as usual. My threadbare brown carpet was as I remembered it. Yet I could still remember just as clearly that bouncy beige towelling carpet in the Starship Dupronic.

At that moment the front doorbell rang. I put my dressing gown on, realising it was eleven thirty, and went to the top of the stairs to hear who it was.

'Oh, it's you dear,' came Auntie's voice loudly and disapprovingly. 'Not more trouble, I hope.'

'No no, Mrs Garden. I just wondered if I could speak to Dominic, please.'

I broke out in a cold sweat. It was Fenella.

'He's asleep. You'd better come back later.' I craned my neck and saw Auntie preparing to shut the door.

'It's all right, Auntie,' I called. 'I'm up. Come on up . . . er . . . Fenella.'

I stood and looked down at the alien in the hall.

'Oh aye?' Auntie watched, disgruntled, from the bottom of the stairs as Fenella ascended, looking ravishing in white shorts and a black t-shirt. She stared back up at me. I felt sweaty and disgusting. My face was spotty and my mouth rancid. I had an urgent need for a large glass of orange juice followed by two strong coffees.

'Good morning, Dominic.'

I pointed towards my room. 'Go in. I'm going to make some coffee. Do you want some?'

Fenella nodded. When I returned with two steaming mugs I found that she had drawn back the curtains, opened the window and made herself at home in my cane chair. Looking at her I found it almost impossible to believe that she was an alien, or that she had been up half the night either. She looked her normal self, pale but cheerful.

'Fenella . . .' I began, and sat down helplessly on the edge of my bed.

'I came to see how you are.' She smiled brightly. 'You didn't seem too well at the disco last night. I went home early because it was so boring. How are you feeling?' As she spoke she raised her right hand and held it out, palm towards me. I looked at it and slowly went cold. 'I thought we could maybe go out and do something different today.' Her tone never faltered. 'You know, let bygones be bygones. What do you think?'

I struggled to find a voice, but for a moment could not speak, any more than I could avert my eyes from the eight pointed black star which seemed engraved into the flesh of her right palm.

'Oh Dominic, I do hope you're not going to sulk,' she continued. While she was speaking she picked up a pen with her left hand – I had never noticed she was left-handed before – leaned over and wrote something on a piece of scrap paper that was lying on my desk. I stood up and looked at it. It said, *We need people like you.*

Twelve

Understanding dawned on me. As it did so I reached out and turned on my radio full blast, looking at Fenella to see if there was any point in doing this, wondering if we could talk if we drowned out whatever was listening and preventing her from speaking freely. Fenella nodded, then removed a small piece of metal from inside one ear and with a slight smile put it next to the radio which was blasting out the latest rock music from Dog-Faced Joe and the Sheepskin Nosebands.

'That'll wake Uncle Simon up,' she mouthed. 'We'll have to talk fast because he'll beep me in a minute. I'm sorry about last night, Dominic. There was simply no alternative. We were being monitored all the time.' She rubbed her eyes, looking tired suddenly. I felt afraid for her, afraid of her, afraid of the whole situation. I lifted her right hand. No sign of the black star remained.

'You're in this . . . Black Star Gang?'

'Yes.'

'The star on your hand, how . . . ?'

'Oh it's like, you know, a hologram, but a million times more advanced. Our scientists can produce mass

60

illusions by the same method, more convincing than anything you can imagine.' She went and stood behind the curtains, watching the Old Rectory. I stood next to her. The postwoman was coming down the lane. A distant tractor moved like a toy towards Blackbarrow Farm. The smell of cut grass came drifting in through the open window. Outside, life was going on as usual and suddenly it all seemed very strange and very precious.

I wondered if the earpiece was beeping yet. There was no way we could hear it above the radio. The music stopped and the presenter's voice came on.

'Well folks, that's Dog-Faced Joe's tenth week at the top of the charts, but will he still be there next week, that's what we'd all like to know, isn't it? My guess is he'll be replaced by Mick Jagger's latest, "Zimmer Rock", rising fast from number thirty last week to number two this week. Now don't forget all those of you who were hoping to see the Russian pop-group Red Sky at Night, at Wembley this evening, the concert has been cancelled. Unfortunately they've been recalled to Moscow because of the worsening international situation . . .'

Fenella frowned and turned back sharply from the window.

'Dominic,' she whispered, 'I don't know what the United Council of Planets is planning for Earth, but we think it's something terrible. I know a lot of people on Earth have to be brain-processed for some reason, including some very important people. I dread to think what it may all be about. I think Uncle Simon and other senior watchers probably know, and one of the reasons the Black Star Gang asked me to apply for this work experience project was to try and find out.'

She paused and wiped a wet coffee ring from my bedside table with the palm that had shown the black star.

'How do you make that . . . illusion . . . come and go?' I asked. It seemed safer somehow to talk about the smaller subject. The larger one, our world peopled by aliens, was simply too frightening.

'Oh, it's controlled mentally. I'll explain more about it later if . . .' She looked at me, then sat down again suddenly in the cane chair. 'Dominic, the Black Star Gang needs more people on Earth, to be ready for whatever happens. There are only two more down here besides me – Mitzalie and her cousin, Claude. Mitzalie is my commander. She's seeing Peter at the moment. Dominic, we don't know you very well yet, but we realised last night that you're probably the sort of person the Black Star Gang needs.'

I sat down and drank some of my coffee. It had gone cold.

'Fenella, you took an awful risk in not processing me last night.'

She raised her eyebrows and nodded.

'It's all risks, all the time. Well, do you want to be part of it?'

I didn't. I knew that very well. She went on.

'If you do, it will be difficult and dangerous. Be in no doubt about that. I spend my entire time absolutely terrified.'

She glanced at the tiny earpiece and reached out to pick it up. I moved more quickly and picked it up first. The same low-pitched beeping which I had heard in the classroom was coming from it in regular bursts. Fenella stood next to the radio and mouthed, 'That means stop whatever it is I'm doing. He doesn't listen in to me all the time but he checks regularly.'

I smiled and shrugged and dropped the earpiece in my coffee.

'Go on with what you were saying. What I'd like to know is why you're not brainwashed. Or are you?'

'Dominic!' Fenella stared in dismay at the tiny row of bubbles rising from the submerged earpiece. She looked up at me and then laughed.

'That gives us about five minutes and then he'll be round here. I'd better make the most of it then.' She turned the radio down. 'No, I'm not brainwashed. None of us in the Black Star Gang is. It all began two years ago in the neighbourhood of a very far off neutron star . . .'

Once upon a time, I thought, and wondered if the world of fairy tales and magic had suddenly reared up and become real and snatched me into its fearsome grip. I wondered if I was imagining all this, or if perhaps I had been brain-processed after all. Fenella was continuing.

'. . . we call them black stars because they don't shine and eventually they turn into black holes. I was aboard the Starship Ashkey with my parents who are programmers. They were on their way to a programmers' conference. Black stars have colossal gravitational pull, you know, and they emit a certain amount of super-powerful radiation. The Ashkey was trapped for three months by the black star's gravity and its radiation threw our computer into complete confusion. It couldn't have processed a rice pudding, let alone a hundred and ten passengers and crew members. People queued up for their monthly processing but there was no point. The computers weren't working. Everyone started to feel very depressed and disorientated without their monthly fix. I can remember how awful I felt. We all said how much we owed the computers for normally sparing us all this. But then after a while we found ourselves having strange, rebellious thoughts, and even voicing them. We started making silly jokes and laughing a lot, despite the danger we were in. Some of us quarrelled and some of us got terribly fond of each other. It was like waking up after not even knowing you had been asleep.'

The doorbell rang. We both jumped.

'I just can't imagine it. It must have been so confusing. I mean, I'm having a spot of bother with reality myself just now, but with that, well you must not have known who you were.'

'Oh, if you think you've ever had a teenage identity crisis you should try that. We felt so shocked at ourselves and at each other, and at the things we were saying. We didn't know whether we were mad or bad or what. But by the end of the three months, when we were rescued, a small group of us knew that we were actually sane for the first time, and that we had a job to do.'

'Oh, Mr Brown,' came Mum's voice from downstairs. 'How nice to see you.'

'So how do you avoid being brain-processed?'

'Nine more of the passengers were programmers, like my parents. We hoped that was enough, if we were all careful to organise our postings and processing points properly, for none of us ever to be brainwashed again. Unfortunately it hasn't been quite that easy and five of us out of the original forty have been lost over the past two years.'

We could hear Uncle Simon's bass tones indistinctly from downstairs. Fenella put her hand in my cup of coffee and fished out the earpiece.

'Dominic,' she said quickly and urgently, 'our aim is to break the United Council of Planets and stop the brainwashing so that people can choose for themselves again. In the meantime we put right whatever we can.'

There were footsteps on the stairs.

'Dominic!' It was Mum's voice. 'Is Fenella there with you? Her uncle wants her.'

'Yes Mum! She's coming!' I yelled back.

'Well Dominic?' Fenella patted the now silent earpiece in a wad of tissues from my bedside table. 'Do you want to help the Black Star Gang?'

A corner of Rupert Bear wallpaper was sticking up by the headboard of my bed. I peeled it off like a last remnant of childhood, and with a head that felt only marginally attached to my body, I nodded.

Thirteen

My parents were pleased that the rift with the Browns was mended. I appeared to have been forgiven for mistaking the ironing board for a corpse, and I apologised profusely to Uncle Simon. He graciously accepted my apology with what I now recognised as the computerised smile of the United Council of Planets.

Peter, Fenella and I went for walks together, and to the cinema, and spent a lot of time in each other's houses. Mitzalie called round several times supposedly in her role as youth contact officer for the local police station. My parents appeared surprised and pleased that we were now so well in with the law, and they took to Mitzalie's relaxed wit in a big way.

That short, peaceful interval between our agreeing to be involved with the Black Star Gang and all hell breaking loose seems like a dream now.

During it, Mitzalie told Peter and myself a lot about the Black Star Gang, including its passwords, 'I believe we met aboard the Starship Ashkey,' to which the reply was, 'No surely it was on the Planet Grockling.' (Grockling, I queried? Doesn't exist, she replied, but there are so many planets that no one's heard of them all.)

She also gave us each a tiny communicator. She and Fenella had two communicators, one for United Council of Planets business and another, a secret one on a secret wavelength, for contacting Black Star members only. Fenella was supposed to leave her UCP communicator on open channel to Uncle Simon at all times, because of her junior position in the watchers project, and he would then beep her if he felt she was making mistakes. She found this intensely annoying. It also meant that we could only talk about Black Star business when he was safely out of range, up on the Starship Dupronic or at the Alpha Centauri Interchange. Fortunately this happened quite frequently.

We were sitting on hay bales in Peter's barn when Mitzalie handed us our communicators. They were fine, soft slivers of metal which fitted deep into the ear channel and were switched on by pulling the earlobe.

'They are for emergency use only,' Mitzalie warned. 'They're programmed verbally by Black Star numbers. You get through to whoever's number you say. You will be BS Eight, Dominic, and you will be BS Nine, Peter. Unfortunately the previous owners of these numbers were lost by being brain-processed. I hope they'll be luckier for you.'

My stomach twisted in what was to be the first of many twinges of apprehension.

Mitzalie also appalled us by her accounts of what the Council had done in the past to recalcitrant planets, such as forcible mass brainwashing, induced famines and earthquakes, alterations to their atmosphere or the addition of tranquillising gases to it.

'I shudder to think what they have lined up for Earth,' she said one day when Fenella, Peter and I had all cycled over to Stoke Stiley and gone to her flat above the delicatessen in the High Street. We had left our bikes propped against the wall outside and bought large vanilla slices in the delicatessen on the way up.

'Really, they should have no power over us,' Peter pointed out, 'since we are not in the planetary council.'

Mitzalie sighed and nodded. 'Well no, but that's never been known to stop them.' She ran her hand through her hair. She had been on night duty and looked shattered. Her hair was greasy and limp and her face puffy.

'You should be asleep in bed,' remarked Fenella. Mitzalie nodded wearily.

'Too right. All this multiple role playing is killing me. Why the UCP had to put me in the police force I can't imagine. I had to be processed with several years' training all in one go. I don't think my brain has recovered yet. I suppose they want people in a position of power to be able to search wherever they want to, for one thing. Frankly I think the UCP will sack me before too long after the feeble excuses I produced for not brain-processing our sergeant and two local chief inspectors.'

She stood up and put the kettle on. Fenella went to the sink and started doing what looked like three weeks' washing up. I felt that in the interests of gender equality I ought to be helping her, but somehow I just didn't.

'The next thing,' said Mitzalie, spooning coffee into the only clean receptacle in the kitchen which happened to be a plantpot holder, 'is to teach these two to fly gravity-blasters. You never know when it might be necessary.'

I sat very still. I had not known that this was part of the deal. I had the terrified feeling that really I ought to learn to drive something earthbound first. I bit into my vanilla slice, trying unsuccessfully to stem the outflow of custard. Maybe I ought to learn to control vanilla slices first. Gravity-blasters went at *how* many parsecs per hour?

Fenella scrubbed vigorously at cementlike traces of ancient food on stacked pots. Outside in the High Street a large lorry hissed its air brakes and a horn sounded. Downstairs in the delicatessen Radio Sixty blasted out rock music. It all seemed rather normal, considering that we were up here talking about flying round the universe.

'There are a few other things too. Altogether it's going to mean several days away from home.' Mitzalie took a pair of police issue black tights from the small washing line above her sink and sieved the coffee through them into the mugs that Fenella had just washed.

I sat forward as she handed me my mug.

'Mitzalie, what will we be doing? What are Peter and I needed for, exactly?'

Mitzalie sat down and smiled at us both.

'Eventually, if you become fully fledged Black Star members, you'll probably want to try and do all the things that the rest of us try and do, stopping the excesses of the United Council of Planets, helping its victims out of trouble. You'll be sent on missions. But for now we just need helpers here on Earth in case of whatever may happen.

'However, you do need to be prepared for any eventualities. You'll need to be processed with the interplanetary language, and in order to go up to the Dupronic where the computers are, we'll need to dye your hair, Peter. I'm afraid that that orangey shade of red is simply unknown in the rest of the galaxy. We'll get one of those easy washout hair colours from Boots. Crimson would be best, I think.'

Peter's jaw dropped. I started to laugh. Helplessly I lay back on the sofa, spitting crumbs and slopping coffee on to my t-shirt. It was a reaction, I suppose, to all the stresses of the past few weeks. By later that day I had begun to feel that there might actually be very little to laugh at.

'If you're to be away for several days we'll have to think of some good reason to give your parents,' Mitzalie concluded.

Fenella raised her wet fingers to her left earlobe.

'A visit to your cousin, Claude?'

The older girl nodded.

Fenella gently tugged at her ear and murmured, 'BS Twenty.'

70

Fourteen

My parents seemed in sombre mood when we had tea in front of the television set later that Saturday afternoon. The early evening news reported the increase in international tension because of Britain's continuing support for the Free Russian Rebels.

'I don't know why we watch the news,' muttered Dad. 'There's never anything cheerful on it. The world seems to have gone mad. It's bad enough that the Russians are getting all militant again, but we're as bad. The prime minister seems set on making matters worse. He appears to have taken leave of his senses, making all these provocative statements.'

'And he seemed such a nice man when we elected him,' complained Mum, passing round the egg and cress sandwiches. 'It's like a complete personality change.'

I paused with my egg and cress sandwich half way to my mouth.

'So where exactly does this cousin Klaus of Mitzalie's live?' asked my mother, switching off the television.

I tried to turn my mind away from the sudden awful thought which had struck me.

'Claude, Mum. Oh, er, he lives in Lancaster.'

'Are you sure he'd want to take all of you lot camping? He must be remarkably good-natured.'

'Er, he helps run an outward bound centre in the Lake District, so he's used to taking people camping.'

'Outward bound? Outward bound? What's that when it's at home then?' shouted Auntie across the room. Maureen the cat went and hid in the wastepaper basket with just her back feet sticking out.

'Is it going to cost much?' asked Dad.

I shook my head. 'Only the train fares. I think Mitzalie's cousin has all the tents and equipment and stuff.'

My parents conferred and nodded.

'Sounds like a good idea,' said Dad. Mum peered at me.

'You don't look very enthusiastic, Dominic. Are you sure you want to go?'

'Oh, er, yes.' I nodded, and went over to sit next to Auntie and explain to her what outward bound meant, whilst trying to drive out the unspeakable thought that had lodged in my brain.

After breakfast the following Monday Fenella, Mitzalie, Peter and I began the train journey north. Mum drove Peter and me to Taunton Station.

'I've got the hair colour,' panted Fenella, only just catching the train after an early morning dash to Boots. 'It should wash out easily afterwards.'

'How did you manage to get away from Uncle Simon?' I asked her. She shrugged.

'I just asked for leave. I said I was homesick, which actually I am. I think he was glad to get rid of me for a while. He thinks I'm several solar systems away at the moment. The advantage is that he won't expect to be able to listen in.'

We caught the new Tyrotrain so we were in Lancaster by mid morning. Mitzalie stuffed the last of a series of snack bars into her cheek – sometimes she reminded me of a large, efficient hamster – and we heaved our rucksacks down from the luggage rack. It was colder up here. Peter and I fastened our para-jackets. A tall fair-haired man approached us as we stepped down from the train.

'Dominic? Peter? How nice to meet you.' He shook us by the hand and hugged Fenella and Mitzalie.

'This is my cousin, Claude,' said Mitzalie.

Claude led us to a Landrover which was parked in the station forecourt and we piled our rucksacks into the back. A sharp wind was blowing grey clouds across the sky. On the hill above us a towering dark castle loomed above the town. We climbed into the Landrover, tucking our hands into our armpits for warmth.

Claude started the engine, revved up and shot jerkily out of the station forecourt. He drove like a maniac through narrow streets into the centre of town, past the bus station, twice round a one-way system, up several steep hills, past a park and finally on to open moorland.

'Lunatic!' yelled a tractor driver as the Landrover

swerved and missed him by a centimetre. 'Where did you come from? A loony bin?'

'Outer space,' bawled Claude over his shoulder.

Young green bracken was curling among last year's blackened stumps on the high treeless moor, and massive grey granite boulders lay in random shifts and falls. Lighter grey sheep, some shorn and some not, standing as still as the boulders, looked at us as we passed. Lambs leapt into the air and ran away. We rumbled bone-shakingly over several cattle grids.

'The North Lancashire Fells,' shouted Claude above the roar of the wind through the open window. 'We're nearly there.'

We turned down a narrow unmade track and after several more minutes of bouncing over stones and tussocks we stopped outside a grey stone farmhouse surrounded by outbuildings. The sun came out and shone behind the hills in long pale streaks. In the distance a glint of blue water showed.

'Morecambe Bay,' Claude pointed as we got out of the Landrover. 'Over the far side you can see the Lakeland Hills.' He opened a five-bar gate and led us through.

Inside, the farmhouse was small but comfortable, sparsely furnished with old furniture and brightly coloured rugs. We dropped our rucksacks and para-jackets in the hall. For a few brief moments I almost began to think we were genuinely going on a camping holiday, but reality returned quickly after lunch. We made brief telephone calls to our parents to reassure them of our safe arrival, then Claude escorted us down a stone-flagged passageway to an open courtyard at the back of the house, past an ancient stone barn with a sagging, moss-encrusted roof and into another, more modern outbuilding. Inside stood two gravity-blasters, one grey and one dark blue.

'Time for a few driving lessons,' announced our host.

I think we both felt that Claude was the last person to be giving driving lessons. I stood back politely to let Peter go first. He gave a sickly grin and climbed into the grey gravity-blaster.

'You watch too, Dominic,' Claude ordered. 'They're very easy to operate. This is the joystick, up, down and side to side. This is revolve into hypervortex which jumps you across space faster than the speed of light . . .' He talked on. I tried to concentrate, but instead of the gravity-blaster's controls I kept seeing before me the strange blank smile on the prime minister's face as he said there would be no turning back.

'Your routes are worked out within the gravity-blaster's computer.' I dragged my attention back to what Claude was saying. 'The computers are on verbal command and will give you almost any information known to humanity, so all you need to know is the name of where you're going. The computer will give you reference co-ordinates . . .'

Our flying lesson went on for two hours, then Peter was allowed to try on his own. He sat confidently at the controls and flicked his fingers over the buttons. Before any of us could jump back, the gravity-blaster hit the ceiling. Fenella closed her eyes as it spiralled slowly back down and came to rest again at our feet.

'Very *good*,' Claude murmured soothingly and helped Peter out. 'Just take it more gently. Now you Dominic.'

I did perhaps a little better, but not much. We practised far into the evening and by supper time Peter and I could fly those gravity-blasters better than Claude could drive his Landrover.

Fifteen

'Now for your disguises.'

We groaned. It was nearly midnight and we were very tired. Claude leaned back against a bale of hay and stretched.

'You'll wear normal interplanetary clothing.' From the top of the hay bales he reached down two pairs of the pyjama-type garments which we had seen on our previous trip into space. Mine were blue, Peter's green.

'Goodnight,' yawned Peter.

Claude did not smile. 'Now one thing you *must* do is to curb your sense of humour. Brain-processed people do not make jokes. When you're supposed to be a good citizen of the galaxy you have to behave like a robot. Above all, do not get angry. Smile at everyone. Ask everyone how they are. Don't argue with those in authority, even justifiably. That implies a questioning attitude. That is one of your weaknesses, Fenella, answering back to Uncle Simon.'

Next came the real fun. Cousin Claude handed out scoot-suits, little engines which strapped on to our backs. These, activated by a switch taped to our left

77

palms, enabled us to fly around the barn as though on invisible microlights. It was terrifying and exciting. The walls came rushing at us and our necks whip-lashed if we stopped too abruptly.

When we had mastered flying inside the barn we flew about outside for a while in the cool, owly night. Fenella put on a scoot-suit too and flew with us.

'This was how I got away from you at the disco,' she grinned.

Silent, pale moths flew towards the lighted barn and a lone bat swooped from the eaves of the house. My thoughts returned to the strange items which had been on the news recently, and to the recent terrible build-up of tension between the nations of the world.

Peter vanished in pursuit of what he declared to be a barn owl and Fenella and I landed in the field behind the barn. Fenella's landing was graceful but I nearly dislocated my ankle.

'Fenella.'

'Yes? Why have we come down here, Dominic?'

'Fenella, I've been having a really alarming thought since yesterday.' We started to walk across the field in the dim starlight. The ground was uneven and slightly boggy underfoot. I wasn't sure how to put this.

'Go on. We'd better carry on flying, Dom, for practice.'

'In a minute. I think to say this I need my feet on the ground. Do you remember when you took me up in your gravity-blaster, before I knew you were in the Black Star Gang, and you said that the United Council of Planets wanted to try and stop us from blowing each other up.'

'I said they wanted to stop you from blowing the rest of the galaxy up.'

I thought for a moment.

'It's not necessarily the same thing,' Fenella added. I looked at her. I could not see her face clearly in the darkness.

'Do you think they might actually want to assist us in blowing each other up?'

'How do you mean?'

'Do you think they might be brain-processing world leaders to make them over-react and behave unreasonably, you know, aggressively towards each other? There have been an awful lot of what seem like ridiculous confrontations recently. Not to mention the really odd happenings, like when the prime minister tap-danced in the House of Commons, and when the German president had amnesia in Marks and Spencer's. I mean, does brain-processing ever go wrong like that?'

We had stopped walking. Fenella's voice was very quiet when she spoke.

'Yes, really large doses of brain-processing can have peculiar side-effects.'

I faced Fenella in the darkness, aware of darkness for the first time as something which could stand between two people, something fearsome and tangible, something which could all too easily be made permanent.

'So do you think that's what they're doing, Fenella? Are the United Council of Planets trying to help us blow ourselves up?'

Fenella took hold of my hand briefly. 'I don't think it's impossible,' she replied.

There was a lot more to learn that night if we were to be convincing aliens. Claude talked and went over plans of the Starship Dupronic. Peter had his hair dyed. As a sleep-addled thrush sounded its first soft mutterings in the rowan tree by the barn door, we learnt to fire the gunlike weapons (which I now found were called incapacitators), on their two functions of 'paralyse' and 'knockout'. I had been in the school rifle club for three years and was already a fair shot. I earned Claude's astonished praise as I knocked Coke can after Coke can off the top of the hay bales. Peter learnt fast too. He had a steady hand and eye after hours at the binoculars.

'You shouldn't need these.' Mitzalie indicated the incapacitators reassuringly. 'It's just part of the training.'

We worked on as more thin birdcalls sounded across the moor and amber light patterned the barn floor. Finally Claude was satisfied.

'Now it just remains for me to give you your official identification,' he yawned, and held out his right hand, palm towards us. Outside, the shrieks of late owls died away into morning. We looked at the black star which seemed to be engraved into his skin. I put out my fingers to touch it. All I felt was skin.

'It's all illusion,' he said. 'I think "black star" and it appears. It will never do so in dangerous circumstances because your unconscious mind won't let it. It's a biometal tattoo and it's activated by your brain. You become able to make other people see it although it isn't really there. It's a form of assisted telepathy.'

Peter was looking doubtful. 'Do we have to have it? My mother said she'd kill me if I ever had a tattoo.'

The tension broke as we all subsided into hysterical laughter.

'Your mother won't see it, Peter.' Mitzalie patted his arm. 'It's for your own protection. It's silent identification when you're not able to give the passwords.'

I did not want to think of circumstances in which one might not be able to give the passwords. Cousin Claude reached down a box from a beam over the loading platform.

'The United Council makes great use of illusions to subdue their enemies. Illusions are so-called kindly weapons. They don't blow your head off, they just make you think you're crazy, and leave no scars. If you're so appalled by what you have seen that you immediately chuck yourself into the nearest river, then that's no concern of theirs. This . . .' he indicated his palm '. . . is one of the few illusions which the Black Star Gang uses. We prefer to keep the lines between pretence and reality well drawn.' He opened the wooden box. 'And this is the biometal marker.'

From the box he produced a heavy-looking black star of such opacity that it seemed more like a hole in the air than an actual object. With what felt like a reflex action I held out my hand and Claude touched the black star to it.

It touched, it burned, then it was gone and no mark

showed. I turned away and went out of the barn into the cold moorland air. Fenella followed me.

'Try it out.'

I thought 'black star' and looked at my hand. Nothing happened.

'You have to think harder,' she said gently. 'Really see it in your mind.'

I really saw it in my mind and then I looked and really saw it on my hand. With wobbly legs I walked away from the barn to the drystone wall which kept the sheep out of the farmyard. A pair of rough, woolly shapes shambled off into the dawn mist which hung in clumps over the longer grass.

We had breakfast at eight and then slept until teatime. By early evening we were on board the Starship Dupronic.

Sixteen

I felt vulnerable, unbelievably naked and vulnerable, walking along those well lit corridors again.

Peter looked horrific, his hair now as crimson as Parry's. He kept saying anxiously that he hoped it would wash out. Our processing had been timed for a shift when none of the spaceship's previous crew would be on duty. Particularly it was essential that Parry should be asleep in her cabin.

None of the faces in the corridors or the computer room were at all familiar, and we saw some aliens such as Strebbit the computer programmer who were of races we had never encountered before. There was a queue for brain-processing, which made it seem more like Sainsbury's than ever. We spoke English to anyone who spoke to us, and they smiled knowingly, obviously assuming that we were on the watchers assignment.

'This is Strebbit.' Fenella introduced a seven foot giant with hooded eyes, as our turn came to step into the metal drawers. Strebbit nodded benignly.

'I believe we met aboard the Starship Ashkey.' His

voice was melodious and fluting. Frantically I racked my brain.

'Er . . . yes . . .' I faltered. 'That is, no, surely it was on the Planet Grockling.' Strebbit grinned charmingly and helped me into one of the drawers.

'OK,' he piped. 'Programming as requested.' His big, flat, sandalled foot gave the drawer a kick and I felt a moment's blind panic in case it was all a terrible mistake. Then I shot backwards into the darkness once more.

This time a clamp came down on my head straight away, and then I had other things to think about, like all the wild, mad voices that were shouting in my head.

What were they saying? What *were* they saying?

Then, I knew.

I woke to find myself sliding back into the bright lights of the computer room.

'What a horrible experience!' Peter was climbing out of his capsule already. 'Honestly Fenella! You never told us it would be like that.'

'Shhh,' she reprimanded.

I opened my mouth for a quiet grumble too, but out came a stream of total gibberish. Yet I understood it, and so did Peter and Fenella.

'I know.' Fenella led us towards the exit. 'You think you'll go mad at first when a new language hits you, don't you.'

We walked out to where Mitzalie was waiting in the corridor, eating a sticky bun. She smiled the Council's plastic smile and led the way back towards the lift. There were three sets of lift doors and all of them were closed. The little digits glowed above them with strange numbers which I now understood, changing as the lifts moved through distant floors of the spaceship. I experimented with talking in the interplanetary language to Peter while we waited. It was an unnerving sensation, knowing something whilst not knowing that you did until the words emerged from your mouth.

It was while we were talking in the interplanetary language that one of the lifts arrived and the lift doors opened. We stepped forward, as you do, giving the people inside room to get out. Then we stopped in our tracks. Inside was a group of fairly human-looking aliens, only recognisable as aliens if one happened to be looking for it. Between them, gripped tightly by his upper arms, was a prisoner trying desperately to wrench himself free. It was Mr Batworthy, our computer teacher.

For a long moment he and I stared at each other, the words of the interplanetary language dying on my lips, then those of us waiting began moving into the lift and the aliens with their prisoner began moving out. I glanced at Peter. He nodded. The lift doors started closing. At the last moment our hands shot out and grabbed Mr Batworthy by his arms and pulled. With a shout his stooped figure stumbled backwards through the narrowing gap, into the lift, his captors taken completely by surprise. They staggered and one of them almost trapped his hand. Then the doors were shut and the lift was moving.

I can't repeat what Fenella said as she stabbed at the buttons. The red digits in the lift flickered and the lift zoomed downwards. By the time the doors opened again at hangar level we all had our incapacitators out and levelled. Dragging a severely shocked Mr Batworthy we ran for the two gravity-blasters. Behind us, another lift arrived.

There was no time to organise ourselves. There were shouts behind us as Peter and I bundled Mr Batworthy into the blue gravity-blaster and fell in after him. As I closed the glass dome, incapacitator beams flickered and the hangar doors began closing. My adrenalin-powered fingers operated the controls as if they had done it all their lives. We skimmed the hangar doors at a sharp angle as they slid slowly towards each other. I saw a glint of metallic grey as Fenella and Mitzalie's gravity-blaster shot over our heads, then we were into hypervortex, spinning out of the restrictions of time and space and heading for home.

Seventeen

Mr Batworthy was clearly too shaken to speak on the journey home. Peter and I were too intent on watching for pursuit. When finally we slowed out of hypervortex and Earth came into view, he moved in his seat and started to look around him. Peter and I had talked in undertones, sometimes in English and sometimes in the interplanetary language.

'It's all right. You'll be all right now,' I had reassured Mr Batworthy once, but then all my attention was taken up again in controlling this small spacecraft. I noticed that Mr Batworthy kept giving me looks of astounded disbelief, and I wished that I could reassure him further, but for now I had to concentrate on getting us safely back to Earth.

'We'd better go back to Claude's, I suppose,' said Peter, as the countries of the world swooped wildly below us. I nodded, asked the computer for the exact co-ordinates and keyed them in.

I felt tense and terrified. I could not believe that I was flying this thing across space. I could not believe that it was within my power to land it safely. The idea had been for both Peter and myself to be closely supervised on our first few flights.

'Now I understand,' croaked Mr Batworthy unexpectedly, 'why you don't always get your homework in on time, Dominic.'

I looked at him and smiled suddenly. I was about to speak but he continued.

'I have to go into hiding. I can't go back to the school. You're not on their side, are you? Those . . . creatures . . . who abducted me?'

I shook my head. 'No Mr Batworthy, we're not on their side.'

Britain appeared below us, just the shape you see it on the weather maps, with dawn creeping across its coastline.

'It's all right. We have somewhere we can take you. We'll talk later.' I concentrated on the controls again.

'Don't forget the radar invisibility screen,' Peter reminded me. I nodded, hovered, dropped, then carefully set us down in the field behind the barn.

I found that my hands were trembling as I finally switched off the power. Peter looked at me with raised eyebrows and a half smile.

'Brilliant,' he said in the interplanetary language. 'And for your next trick?'

Moments later Fenella and Mitzalie's gravity-blaster landed behind us and Claude came rushing out of the farmhouse in his pyjamas, real flannelette striped ones from Marks and Spencer's this time. Mr Batworthy looked terribly alarmed, his face pale in the dawn light.

'Who are you really?' he whispered in a terrified voice.

'It's all right, honestly,' I told him. 'You're safe. You've been rescued by the Black Star Gang. I don't know what happened to you, but we'll go in and sit down and then you can tell us all about it.'

Two hours later, after coffee and orange juice and cornflakes and toast, we sat silently and considered what we knew.

It seemed that Mr Batworthy had been snatched from the school computer room where he had been working late on a new program.

'Do you know why they took you?' I asked him. He folded his arms across his chest and glanced away out of the window.

'It may be connected with something I've been working on.' His tone was evasive.

'The hypo-relativity syndrome.'

For a moment I thought he was going to have a heart attack. I wished I had spoken more cautiously.

'You . . . know . . . ?' he stammered.

'I take it you haven't written it up for any of the scientific journals yet, or told anyone else about it? You see, they want to stop you, to erase your memory before you can share your discovery with anyone else. They want to stop any of us on this planet from travelling into space.'

Mr Batworthy just stared at me. He seemed to struggle for words. 'Who else knows . . . about my discovery, Dominic?'

I glanced at Mitzalie. 'All the aliens, I think. No-one

else on Earth except for Peter and me. But there is an American scientist who has also discovered the same formula for travelling faster than light.'

Mr Batworthy's expression became animated. 'Joe Chapman? Has he? I knew he was close . . .'

Mitzalie interrupted. 'We were too late for him,' she said. Her voice was sombre. 'They found him in his laboratory making paper chains out of his computer printouts. He has no idea what relativity is now. He doesn't even know what time it is.'

'I'm sorry, Silas.' Claude stood up and put his hand on Mr Batworthy's shoulder as the older man sank his head into his hands. 'You'd better stay here for the time being. It's isolated and safe, and I find that sheep farming is a good cover for whatever I want to do. I'll give you a room to work in and you can try and get used to my computers. The quickest way of ensuring your own safety is to publish your findings, now. It won't be worth their while wiping your mind after that. Are you at the point where you can?' Claude raised his eyebrows.

Mr Batworthy nodded, his face lighting up briefly at the word 'computers'.

'It will be difficult, without all my papers and equipment, but I shall have to try.'

Later that day Fenella, Mitzalie, Peter and I caught the train home.

Eighteen

It was wonderful but unsettling to be back home. We had a crisis with Peter's hair because the bright red hair colour would not all wash out.

'Perhaps it's the sun, Mum,' he said sheepishly when first confronted by his mother's incredulous stare. We all stood on the platform at Taunton Station. In the end, though, he had to admit that yes, he had indeed dyed his hair.

Mrs Baxendale and my mother slid horrified glances at each other. Their we-must-try-and-understand-teen-agers expressions almost came unstuck for a few seconds, then, heroically, they recovered.

'On a *camping* holiday? However did you manage it?' murmured Mrs Baxendale in unnaturally casual tones.

'Oh Mum.' Peter sounded tired. 'It's rather a long story.' His mother looked at his face and was silent, but I had the feeling that he had not heard the last of it.

'That Peter Baxendale!' squeaked Auntie in the privacy of our own car on the way back home. 'What a sight he looked and no mistake. Red hair! Huh! What does he think he is? A punk? A Communist? He'll come to no good with red hair, you mark my words. Don't you go dyeing *your* hair, Dominic. It's bad enough when lasses do it.' She stared accusingly at Mum who sometimes blended her grey bits in. 'If God had intended us to dye our hair he'd have put paint-brushes in our ears. I don't know what the world's coming to.'

I sat back and closed my eyes. Auntie's words buzzed in my head as the desire to sleep swept over me. I feared that in the days to come not just Auntie, but all of us, might not know what the world was coming to.

In the house everything looked tidier than normal. Perhaps it was because I had not been there to mess it up. The kitchen smelt of cakes and apples. The normality was almost too much.

Julia came rushing to meet me. 'Hi Dominic! You look different. How was the camping? Did you fall off any mountains?' She hugged me and I felt uncharacter-istically touched.

I was even more touched when Dad announced that he was opening a bottle of wine at dinnertime that evening to celebrate my homecoming. It was most unlike Dad to evince any sort of gladness at one's presence, even when he felt it.

He had a litre bottle labelled 'full-bodied red' from the County Stores, and he poured me a glassful.

'Just the one, Dominic, to celebrate,' he added warningly, in case I was thinking of becoming an alcoholic. Julia was not even allowed that.

Everybody else was soon on their second glassful and Auntie was soon on her third.

'It's a long time since we've had Ribena,' she remarked as she held out her glass once more.

'It's *wine*, Auntie,' enunciated Mum clearly, leaning towards Auntie's ear. Auntie looked startled.

'Well why didn't you say so, Geraldine? I shall be as legless as a rat before the harvester.'

I paused with a forkful of steak halfway to my mouth. Auntie's agricultural imagery sometimes stunted one's appetite.

As the second course, icecream with chocolate flakes, followed, I talked about my imaginary mountain climbing. I included as much of the truth as I could. I told them about Claude's crazy driving, the view of the bay, the sheep and the long, rolling fells.

'I thought you would have more of a sun tan, Dominic,' said Mum, helping me to more icecream. 'The weather up there was supposed to be quite good.' With an unthinking gesture she refilled Auntie's proffered glass once more. Auntie beamed and swayed in her chair. Saving me from having to explain my lack of a sun tan, the doorbell rang.

'I'll go, Mum,' I said, but Auntie was already on her feet too and halfway down the hall, her wineglass slopping wine all up her arm.

'It'll be Mrs Pruitt about the Women's Institute,' she shouted over her shoulder, her voice indistinct.

'You'd better go after her.' Mum half rose. I nodded and followed Auntie down the hall.

'It's all right, Auntie. You go back and eat your icecream before it melts.' But Auntie was already pulling the door open, swaying backwards with it as it swung. A woman stood on the step with her back to us. She wore a smart tweed suit, and her dark brown hair was pulled back into a bun so severe that it seemed in danger of scalping her. She turned towards us and smiled.

'Good evening,' she murmured, crinkling her eyes up into a confidential smile. It was Parry.

Nineteen

It seemed a long moment, while we looked at one another, and Parry's eyebrows rose in polite query, but in real time it was probably no more than a couple of seconds.

'Jehovah's Witnesses?' demanded Auntie aggressively.

'Oh no, and I do apologise for disturbing you.' I saw Auntie casting incredulous glances at the newcomer's far-spaced, outward-staring eyes, then down disbelievingly at the glass of wine in her hand. 'I'm a social worker,' Parry was continuing, 'and I'm looking for one of my clients who has gone missing . . .'

'Oh. Oh aye.' Auntie glanced quickly back up at the visitor's face, clearly feeling that she might have phrased this better.

I stood transfixed to the spot, my mind churning in confusion. Parry was giving no signs of recognition, so she must obviously still think that I had been brain-processed as intended. There was no reason for her to associate me with Mr Batworthy's rescuers. I was therefore still safe, my cover intact, unless . . . unless I had given myself away by my expression of shock.

I allowed myself a breathing space by bending down to stroke Perkin who had come swinging down the hall with his usual swagger.

'This client who is missing is a very disturbed person.' Parry also stooped to stroke the cat, but Perkin flattened his ears and backed away. 'He's a poor, poor man really, quite ill. He needs help. Lots of help. I wonder if anyone here might have seen him? He's very tall with a pale complexion, almost greenish really because he suffers from Mexican jaundice. It's essential that we find him, because he could be dangerous, so we're making enquiries from door to door.'

Auntie steadied herself against the doorpost and took another reassuring sip from her glass. 'Well I haven't seen him.' She looked away hurriedly and started humming to herself as the alien caught her staring at her eyes again.

'I'm afraid I haven't seen him either,' I added. 'I'll ask if anyone else has.' As I walked back down the hall, my brain struggled with this development. Tall? Greenish? Could it be that the Myrions were here again and that Parry was hunting them down, poor things?

'Anyone seen a tall, green, disturbed social misfit?' I enquired round the living room door. Dad, Mum and Julia gave astonished shakes of the head. When I returned to the front door Auntie was chatting to the stranger.

'We're celebrating my nephew's return,' she said, indicating her glass of wine which was now almost empty again since most of it had landed on the cat. 'Been right away, he has. Return of the prodigal. Says he's been up some mountains, but ain't got no sun tan.'

'I'm sorry we can't help you,' I said, starting to close the door. 'No-one here has seen anyone at all like your client. I'm so sorry.'

'Oh well, thank you . . .'

I closed the door completely then, but at the last moment, as the crack narrowed, I saw a strange frown cross Parry's face.

My icecream had melted and I didn't want to stay at the table for cheese and biscuits. Why oh why had Auntie had to make those last remarks? On their own they might have meant nothing, but combined with my own expression of shock at seeing Parry, they could just have been enough to arouse the alien commander's suspicions. I excused myself from the table.

'I'm going to have a bath, Mum,' I said. 'I haven't had one since I left.' Julia held her nose and I attempted the required brotherly sneer.

In the bathroom I switched on my communicator.

'BS Eight to BS Fourteen,' I whispered, below the roar of hot water and steam.

'Hi.' Fenella's voice came straight away. 'What are you doing?'

'Having a bath and shaking with fright.' I sat down on the pine towel chest. 'I've just had a visit from Parry.'

There was a short, shocked silence.

'*What?*' breathed Fenella.

'She's here. It sounds as though the Myrions are back and she's searching for them.'

'Oh no! What did you do? You're not supposed to know her. Did you give yourself away?'

'I'm not sure. I may have. I . . . think I looked shocked when I saw her, but she could put that down to her unusual appearance. But then Auntie said that I had been away for a while.'

Fenella paused. 'That could well be enough for Parry. Where is your incapacitator?'

'In my locked desk drawer.'

'Put it in your shoulder holster, now.'

'Good grief, what do you think may happen, F . . . BS Fourteen?'

'They may try to snatch you, just to be on the safe side, and have you, as they think, reprocessed. You'd better contact BS Nine and warn him that Parry is here, in case she calls on him too. I'll contact BS Thirty. Do be careful.'

'BS Fourteen . . .'

'Yes?' Her voice was tense. I hesitated.

'If Parry does suspect me, then it will only take her a few simple deductions to start suspecting you too. After all, you were supposed to have brain-processed me. We'd better have no contact for a while.'

There was another pause.

'I don't think there's much point in that, BS Eight. It's too late. Anyway there are some things I must give you. Can you meet me outside?'

'Yes, probably.'

'Leave the bathroom door locked and the radio on, or

something. Then if Parry calls back you'll be unavailably in the bath. Can you climb down from your bathroom window?'

'I can try.'

'Good. Don't break your neck. I'll see you in your garden shed.'

'OK.'

'Bring your incapacitator.'

'Right.'

I turned the taps off and put one of Auntie's Beatles discs at full blast on my laser player – Auntie tended to behave as though she had personally invented the legendary 1960s of her childhood and she loved it when Julia and I borrowed her old recordings. Then I pushed open the bathroom window.

'Too loud!' yelled Dad from downstairs.

'Sorry Dad,' I called back and turned the music down. 'Hey *Jude*, don't make it *bad* . . .' I hummed with the music for a moment, and sighed. Then with my whereabouts well and truly established, I climbed out of the bathroom window, slid down the drainpipe and padded barefoot across the back lawn to our tumbledown wooden garden shed.

Twenty

The shed was full of bicycles. Each of us in the family had one, even Auntie, but only Julia and I ever rode them. The last time the elders had been on an exercise binge, Auntie had ridden hers into a hedge and broken her glasses. Now the bikes stood festooned in spiders' webs and dulled with the damp skin that precedes rust. Plantpots and garden tools surrounded them. My and Julia's racers, however, were a different matter. They stood near the door and gleamed. I could see them through the dusty glass, powerhouses of moonlit carbon.

I went in through the creaky door. A dark figure rose from behind the lawnmower like a shadow. My heart nearly stopped.

'Hi,' whispered Fenella. I shuddered with relief. She indicated that I should join her in the corner where heaps of flowerpots lay drunkenly against the wall. She sat back down on a broken upturned tub, making space for me next to her.

'Dominic, I'm glad you could get here.' We sat shoulder to shoulder in silence for a moment while my eyes adjusted to the darkness and we watched each other's expressions grow visible in the gloom. Fenella's gave me no reassurance at all. She took my hand suddenly.

'Let's look on the black side,' she said. 'We'll assume that Parry really is suspicious of you. It may mean that you have to go on the run for a while . . .' She saw my look of dismay. 'Don't worry. If you have to vanish for long I'll just have to tell your parents enough of the truth to make them understand. Anyway, I want you to have some of our special gadgets. They're strictly limited issue for special needs, as they're very expensive to produce. Our leader, BS One, makes the gadgets at night in a United Council laboratory, taking the most dreadful risks.'

Fenella switched on a pencil-beam torch and shone it into her canvas school bag which lay on the floor at her feet.

'I have my doubts about the value of this . . .' She dug her hand in and produced a copper bracelet, '. . . but it can sometimes give you a few precious minutes to escape.' She held it out to me. 'Put it on.'

I took the bracelet and wriggled my rather large hand through it. Nothing happened. In the dim moonlight I could see that Fenella was laughing.

'Lovely.'

'What is it supposed to do?' I asked in irritation. I was definitely not in the mood for games. With a squeamish expression which I did not at the time understand, Fenella removed the bracelet from my wrist and put it on to her own. I recoiled with a startled gasp. I could feel my hair literally standing on end and the flesh creeping on my bones. Where Fenella had been sitting, a hideous fluorescent monster with black teeth now towered up to the ceiling.

Then she was back, the bracelet held out on her palm.

'Dear God.' I could hardly speak. 'That isn't what you really look like, is it, Fenella?'

She doubled up with laughter. 'No, no, don't worry, this is the real me. You should have seen yourself though. I'm not sure if it wasn't an improvement . . .'

I smiled reluctantly. Fenella picked up the copper bracelet again. 'It works by refracting your molecules. It leaves you with a dreadful headache, so it's better to keep it just for dire emergencies.' She delved into her bag again and I closed my eyes and breathed deeply for a moment. 'Now these are much more useful. We call them ultrasonics.' She took out a handful of small white plastic frisbees. 'They knock people temporarily unconscious by a brief alteration in their brain waves. They cause a different level of consciousness rather like being asleep. It's actually rather pleasant. Your Black Star communicator has a built-in protector so that you are not affected when you use them. They leave people out cold for about an hour. You prime them with this button, then just throw them. Be careful never to use them in traffic though.

'Now this . . .' She took out of her bag a thickly folded sheet of polythene. 'You must be very careful with this. It's a gravity blanket, and there's a definite knack to using it. Open it too fast and you'll find yourself flat on your face. You need a quick flick of the wrist and it pins your enemy to the ground.' Fenella shook the polythene partly open, but instead of floating lightly on the air, it seemed to increase in weight, and flopped heavily against her legs, almost dragging her to her knees. Garden implements clanked as she staggered.

'Ouch. Not a very good demonstration. You see its weight increases the further you open it. Fully open it weighs half a ton. You can practise with it in a moment.'

Next out of the bag she produced a torchlike instrument. 'You'd better have this. It's a standard issue Council daylight probe. These things which look like sunglasses are night specs. You can see in the dark. And here's the body belt they all fit into. It goes on like this, diagonally over the shoulder and under the arm, the opposite way from the incapacitator holster. OK?'

I nodded.

'Good. We'll have a little practice with them now, and then you'd better get back to the house before you're missed.'

Half an hour later, with my gadgets in their body belt and my black sweater over the top, I tiptoed across the lawn. Fenella came with me to the back of the house.

'Be careful, Dominic. Don't forget that using any of these weapons apart from the daylight probe reveals you instantly to the Council's agents as a member of the Black Star Gang, so only use them if you have to.'

We stood by the wall. I felt desperately afraid. Fenella kissed me briefly on the cheek and then she was gone.

I stared after her for a moment, then clumsily started

to climb back up the drainpipe towards the lighted bathroom window, toying with the idea of simply going round to the front door and walking in, but deterred by the thought of Parry maybe lurking in the bushes.

Finally I reached the open casement window, resisted the temptation to look down and heaved myself over the ledge. The cream towelling curtains wrapped themselves round my head and my foot skidded in the slippery washbasin. Carefully I eased myself over the soaps and toothbrushes and into the steam-filled room. It was only then that I became aware that someone was standing outside, hammering on the locked bathroom door.

Twenty-one

It was my father. He sounded as if he were about to have a fit.

'Dominic!' he was bellowing. 'Open this door at once! I know you're in there. I shall have to break the door down. Is something the matter? Are you ill? Open this door at once!'

I opened the door. I had no alternative really, despite my fully clothed state and muddy feet. I knew by the tone of his voice that my father was quite capable of breaking the door off its hinges, particularly if he'd been watching too many American gangster films.

'Hi, Dad.'

My father stood with his fist raised, his expression of anger quickly dissolving into one of bewilderment and anxiety.

'Dominic.'

He stepped into the bathroom and looked from my dishevelled and slightly cobwebby appearance, to the scrape marks in the washbasin, then at the crystal-clear water swaying in the bath. He stifled a smile.

'Humphrey?' Mum's voice called anxiously from the bottom of the stairs. 'Is he all right?'

Dad turned back. 'Yes dear. He's fine. I'll be down in a minute.' Then he came back and sat down on the towel chest. Suddenly weak at the knees – suppose he noticed my strangely bulging torso – I sank down on to the edge of the bath. I realised in that moment the toll that my recent adventures were taking of me. It must be beginning to show, in my face, in my voice, in a tiredness and wariness that I could sense but not control. I tried to relax the stressful set of my shoulders. Dad gave me a long look, then he patted me on the knee.

'Dominic, I do understand.'

I doubted it. He unrolled a strip of toilet paper and started to clean the mud from the washbasin. His eyes flicked back to mine.

'Don't think I haven't noticed how things are with you lately.' He gave an airy laugh. 'I'm not blind, you know. And we've all been through it. Do you want to talk about it?'

I could feel my glazed expression. Oh yeah Dad. The planet's been invaded by aliens. Nothing too serious, you understand. They only want to computerise our brains and make us good.

'Dad? I don't quite understand what you mean.' I felt I might go mad if this were to be another of Dad's little lectures on the facts of life. Did the adult world think that life contained no other facts besides these? How did they ever get anything done?

'Teenage love, Dominic.' He shook his head and

inhaled ruefully through his teeth. 'It's never been easy. We know how you feel about Fenella, and I can see that there might be something rather romantic about climbing out of a window to meet her, but your mother and I are worried that you feel you need to keep it so secret. You've never been like this with your other girlfriends . . .' I thought of Louise and Susan, brief involvements which seemed like another lifetime. I couldn't even remember their faces.

'Dad . . .'

'Oh I know.' He gave a worldly grimace. 'You think you know it all and it's none of my business. Just remember you've got important exams next year and there's more to life than girls, Dominic. Keep things in perspective. Cool it.' (The Beatles disc was still playing and seemed to be affecting his vocabulary.) 'Try and keep things casual. It's not the end of the world, you know.'

I tried to stop it, but laughter welled up inside me, hysterical releasing laughter. I laughed until tears ran down my cheeks, and Dad laughed too.

'That's the spirit, Dominic. Have a good laugh. As long as you can laugh at yourself you'll be all right.'

He gave me a clap on the shoulder and turned to go.

'Oh, I forgot what I came up to say in the first place. There's somebody here to see you. He says he's doing a survey of teenage attitudes, and someone recommended you as being very articulate. He'd like to interview you. It seems a bit late but I said I'd ask you.'

I felt as though I had been punched in the stomach.

'Dad, I can't just now . . . I just don't feel . . .'

x

Auntie tottered past the open door with Maureen purring at her heels. They both looked extremely unsteady on their feet. There was a rolled-up copy of *The Independent* under Auntie's arm.

'I'm going to bed, Humphrey. I suppose it's too much to ask to use the bathroom?' Her enunciation was not helped either by the County Stores' full-bodied red, or by the fact that she held her false teeth in her hands behind her back.

'We won't be long, Auntie,' Dad replied in soothing tones. Maureen came in and jumped on to the edge of the bath beside me.

'Hello Moron,' I murmured fondly. Her purring increased until it sounded like the blowing of multiple raspberries. On the steam-slippery surface one of her back legs shot out from under her and landed in the now rapidly cooling water. With a howl the startled cat crashed to the floor and lay there motionless, her wet leg in the air. Auntie rushed to pick her up, dropping her newspaper. Briefly I saw the main headline 'Crisis deepens with exchange of insults between Kremlin and Whitehall', then my eyes went to a smaller headline next to a photograph of President Chestikov of Russia. 'Russian president speaks to Congress of Party Deputies in unknown language'. Edging past Auntie and the wet cat, I took advantage of the confusion and slipped away.

'I'm going to bed, Dad,' I called as I fled. 'Tell the man to interview someone else. I don't have any attitudes at the moment.'

My own room at the end of the landing beckoned

welcomingly. I raced in, slammed the door and wedged a chair securely under the handle.

For half an hour I listened apprehensively to the sounds of the rest of the house. I heard my mother talking apologetically to someone, then the front door opening and shutting. Maybe the visitor really had been a researcher, I reflected. Maybe I had missed the opportunity of becoming a spokesman for modern youth. But somehow I didn't think so. It was too much of a coincidence after Parry's visit. One thing was certain though. If it had been a Council agent, he wasn't going to give up that easily. I glanced nervously towards my window. What was there to stop someone coming in during the night and spiriting me three galaxies away by morning? Or worse still, having me back in bed with a blanked-out mind in the space of a couple of hours. I began to realise, with growing certainty, that I would have to spend the night hiding somewhere away from home. Just then a faint buzz, like a very small bluebottle, sounded in my left ear.

'BS Nine to BS Eight.' It was Peter.

I sat down on my bed.

'Hello.'

'Hello BS Eight. Listen, have you had any visitors? Since Parry, I mean?'

I answered him as softly as I could.

'Yes. A so-called researcher. I refused to see him.'

'Is that all?'

'It was enough. I'm rapidly becoming paranoid.'

'BS Eight, we've got worse trouble than that. You remember your corpse in the cupboard?'

'Rather well.'

'He's here.'

'*What*?'

'He's here, in the room with me, sitting on my bed.'

'Good grief.'

'He's stolen my incapacitator and my scoot-suit. He says he needs them to get away. He says Parry is after him. He also has a friend, a Myrion woman. He says she's coming over to ask you for your incapacitator and scoot-suit.'

At that moment two things happened. A knock came at my bedroom door.

'Dominic?' It was Auntie's quavery voice.

And my wardrobe door swung open.

Twenty-two

If I learnt nothing else that night, I learn that chairs under doorhandles do not keep out determined great-aunts. She and the Myrion woman both tumbled into my room at the same moment.

The odd thing about the Myrions is that they look so close to human, and yet are different enough to be disconcerting. Their height, about six foot six and upwards, isn't unheard of here, and their pallor with its greenish tinge only looks like that of someone who is extremely ill. It's the two in combination which give the Frankenstein effect, and it became clear that Auntie, as she slowly froze to a halt, knew a monster when she saw one. She and the alien woman stared at each other for a long, long moment.

'Oh-h-h . . .' said Auntie finally in a tiny voice. 'Dominic? I think I've had too much to drink.' She frowned in peevish rage. 'Dominic, that wine must have been contami . . . nami . . . aminaminated!' She sat down hard in my cane chair and with the fingers of her right hand tried to pinch the skin of her left hand, but missed and pinched the sleeve of her blue dressing gown instead. A relieved smile spread across her face.

'Oh *that's* all right then. This must be a dream, Dominic. I'm pinching myself but I can't feel a thing.' She leaned forward confidentially. 'You know, Dominic, I'm seeing something really strange.' She gave a nervous laugh. 'You should be glad you're not having this dream, lad.'

'Yes, Auntie.'

The Myrion woman shrugged her huge, green, American-football-player shoulders apologetically. 'Just give me your incapacitator and your scoot-suit and I'll go,' she said in the interplanetary language. Auntie sat bolt upright in her chair.

'It's gibbering!' she cried. 'It's talking Double Dutch, Dominic!'

'I don't understand you, I'm afraid,' I said carefully to the Myrion woman in English.

'I should think not!' exclaimed Auntie. An irritated frown crossed the alien's face.

'Oh come on. I know you're one of the Ashkey fighters.' She held out her hand impatiently and flicked her huge gherkin fingers. I felt a shiver of alarm that this unreliable person knew of our connection with the Starship Ashkey and therefore part of our password. It would only need the UCP to check the passenger lists ... I made a mental note to suggest it should be changed.

'Ashkey? Ashkey?' Auntie picked out the word from the garble of syllables. 'Oh God bless you! The poor monster has a cold, Dominic.'

112

'We're on your side,' the Myrion continued in an exasperated voice, 'but my husband and I have to get away. Council agents are after us. Commander Parry is right on our tail and she'll have us in her computers as soon as look at us. We've lost all our equipment in a gravity-blaster crash in Neroche Forest. Just help us get away. Surely the Black Star Gang has plenty more incapacitators and scoot-suits? We only came here to try and help your stupid planet in the first place. We thought we could embarrass the Council's watchers into giving up.'

I felt a twinge of sympathy and glanced at Auntie. Then I replied to the green woman in the interplanetary language. Auntie leaned forward very slowly, her mouth dropping open.

'You don't understand,' I said quietly, belatedly closing the bedroom door after moving Maureen's prostrate form from the threshold. 'I'm in trouble too. I have to get away. Parry's after me as well. I can't stay here tonight, and I may need my incapacitor and scoot-suit myself later.'

'Look, just give them to me for now, and I'll help you too one day.' She began roughly opening drawers and rummaging through my clothes. I began to see what made Parry so keen to process Myrions. In the bottom drawer the woman found my scoot-suit.

'OK, we'll compromise.' She stood up straight, holding it. 'I'll have the suit. You keep the incapacitator . . .' But she never finished what she was going to say because Auntie launched herself across the room and smashed her across the chest with her hot water bottle.

The Myrion crashed to the floor like the curse of the Mummy's tomb and Auntie wrenched the scoot-suit triumphantly out of her hands.

'Don't you take my nephew's things!' she bellowed, waving the scoot-suit above her head. 'What *is* this, Dominic?' She examined the little control box in her hand, and started to slide the button along.

'*No* Auntie! Don't press . . .' It was too late. With a jerk Auntie soared into the air.

'BS Eight?' It was Peter's voice in my ear. 'Are things all right over there? What's happening?'

My voice came out in a hollow contralto. 'No BS Nine, things are not all right. A Myrion lady has fallen out of my wardrobe and my great-aunt is cruising at fifteen hundred feet above sea level.' How could I be so flippant? I hated myself for it sometimes and decided it was a bad habit I would concentrate on getting rid of later, assuming that I survived to get rid of my own bad habits rather than having them all erased in one go by Parry.

I looked up at Auntie. She was swooping jerkily around the room emitting little whoops of shock and delight as she fiddled with the controls in her vein-ridged hands. Her legs flailed and her slippers fell off one by one.

'Oh. I see.' Peter paused. The calmness induced by a lifetime's birdwatching is a wonderful thing. 'Well there's not a lot I can say to that, BS Eight.'

My reply was muffled because at that moment Auntie fell on my head. We both collapsed on to my bed, and by the time I had managed to sit up again, the Myrion woman and the scoot-suit had gone.

Auntie now appeared to be in a peaceful alcoholic doze. She lay, star-shaped, pink pyjamaed and blue dressing gowned, on my purple and navy quilt. I straightened her out and put her slippers back on her feet.

'BS Nine?' I whispered. 'I'm getting out of here. Too many people are after me. I'm going to hide in the loft over the village hall for tonight. Maybe you should come and join me there.'

'Yes. You're right. My Myrion has just gone.'

'Mine too. I'll just put Auntie to bed. Twenty minutes?'

'I'll be there.'

I poked my head out of the door. Julia was heading for the bathroom in her fluffy red slippers.

'Hi Dom. Finished in here?'

'Yes thanks.' The sheer normality of my little sister threatened to blow me apart. When she had gone, and the bathroom door was safely closed, I dragged Auntie along the landing to her own bed. She was surprisingly light. I tucked her in, still in her dressing gown, and planted a kiss on her soft, corrugated cheek.

'Good night, Auntie.'

One thin hand twitched on the bed covers and she smiled in her sleep. She was all right.

I returned to my room, adjusted my belt full of gadgets, took my incapacitator from my desk and for the second time that night climbed out of an upstairs window.

Twenty-three

I had not anticipated there being a function on at the village hall. Bright lights shone out of the windows. The car park was full. What was it? I racked my brains. Women's Institute? Mothers' Union? An evening class? Most likely a private function of some kind. As I drew nearer I could hear music faintly from inside.

Peter and I met below the broken oriel window which led into the hall's boarded loft. We had often climbed up there in years gone by. Not many other people seemed aware of the loft's existence, as the sides of the hall were densely covered in virginia creeper and the window was not obvious. We had found, when we were children and the whole thing had seemed very exciting, that knot holes in the wooden floor of the loft and cracks in the crumbling plaster ceiling below gave good views down into the hall at certain points. This had seemed to have terrific potential at one time, but experience had shown us that most of what went on in the hall was so boring that it was not worth the trouble.

We climbed up the gnarled sturdy branches of the virginia creeper. The little window had remained unmended for as long as I could remember. People were always complaining about the draughtiness of the village hall, but I think that only Peter and I knew the reason for this.

At the top I clung on while Peter pulled himself mincingly through. Small sharp slivers of glass still protruded from the paintless circular frame. The leaves of the virginia creeper were bottle green in the darkness. By September they would be scarlet. Where would we all be by September?

The leaves quivered horizontally in a slight breeze as I eased myself through after Peter. Inside in the darkness pale sunshine-starved tendrils crept across the dusty boards. The roofspace was filled with a damp smell. Through the floorboards came pinpricks of golden light. I switched on my torch.

'We may not sleep much, but at least we should be safe here,' Peter whispered as we crawled across the splintery floor. Swathes of spiders' webs brushed our faces. Peter crouched down and peered through one of the knot holes. After a moment he gave a quiet laugh. 'Come and have a look. It's the annual teachers' rave.'

I crept through the webby gloom and put my eye to a neighbouring knot hole. He was right. I suppressed a grin. It was the National Union of Teachers' barn dance. I sat back on my heels. Peter shifted to get a better view.

'I feel worse about doing this than I used to,' he muttered. 'Nevertheless I think we have a public duty to see what scandals we can uncover. Oh excellent, it's Rocking Rupert with . . .' His voice died. I was holding

117

my torch in my mouth and prising a small splinter of glass from my left palm. What could Mr Rupert, our biology teacher, be doing to cause such horrified stillness in Peter? I tilted my head back, moving the torch beam upwards so that I could see Peter's face as he sat up. He looked spectral in the dim light.

'What is it?'

Peter pointed wordlessly to the hole in the floor. I shuffled over towards him, dust marking my black jeans like photographic negatives. The music and laughter sounded louder as I lay flat on my stomach. I focussed my right eye on the long crack around the wood knot. I could just see a narrow section of the room. Ms Tuttle frisked into view then out again.

'Now swing your pardners rewnd and rewnd,' tannoyed the caller. Mr Rupert twirled Ms Tuttle rewnd and rewnd with lecherous glee, then the other couple of the foursome came into view. Half of it was Livia Bunch, our German teacher and organiser of social events, in her ethnic skirt and yakskin boots. The other half – a long cold shiver travelled across my back – was Uncle Simon.

I sat up.

'It may mean nothing. He may just be expanding his social life.'

Peter shook his head and crouched back down. 'Somebody must have brought him. Probably Livia. People can only come if they're brought by one of the teachers. He and Livia seem to know each other awfully well, too. Look.'

I looked back through my knot hole. He was right.

The two couples were holding hands now and jogging in and out as the music changed key. Livia leaned over and said something and Uncle Simon threw back his head and laughed uproariously.

We watched them for a long time. When finally we sat up I stood my torch on end so that its beam shone towards the roof.

'If Livia's one of them too, then who else may be? How on earth are we going to know who's safe to trust? We're going to have to be awfully careful not to give ourselves away. They're bound to be on the lookout for Mr Batworthy's rescuers, as well as for Mr Batworthy.'

Peter bent down and looked through the crack again, then sat quickly up. 'They're going out. We'd better follow them.'

We switched off our torches then shuffled back across the boards to the oriel window. I had one leg out already when I realised that Livia and Uncle Simon were now standing directly below us in the darkness outside the village hall. I stilled Peter with my hand and we listened. Their voices were just audible on the warm night breeze. With the utmost caution I eased my leg back in and released a shaky breath. Then we huddled down to hear what they were saying.

'. . . so glad you're here, Simon . . .' It was Livia's voice. She spoke the interplanetary language. So that was that then. Peter and I exchanged glances. 'I've told all the other staff members that you're my cousin.'

Their voices dropped for a moment then became audible again.

'You may be right about Batworthy's accomplices

being from Earth, Simon. They could even be in the school. I gather from Parry that you had no luck with your researcher.

'No, none at all. Such apathy in the young makes me realise just how much this planet needs us. Half of them didn't even want to see him.'

A wave of fright smashed over my head. Despite my suspicions of the 'researcher into teenage attitudes', it was a shock to have them confirmed. I could have been in a computer having my brain wiped clean at this very moment.

A floorboard creaked behind us. I half turned, frowning at Peter to be quiet. But he was here next to me. Something like the faintest sigh of air touched my neck. I saw Peter stiffen. The air shifted again, and again there was the soft moan of resistant wood.

'Oh well,' Livia was saying, 'perhaps Parry will have more luck. She seems very confident now she has the Black Star communicator.

'She went off saying she knew exactly where they were going, and that she would be there waiting for them.'

The hairs on the back of my neck rose with a slow, horrid precision. Peter and I turned, raising our torches. We switched them on and swept the beams across the far, dark recesses of the loft. Dust motes hung in the looping arcs of light.

She was sitting on a crossbar of the rafters in the farthest corner of the loft. Her tweed suit was smeared with dust. Her incapacitator was held in two hands which were steadied by the support of her elbows on her knees.

'Hello Dominic. Hello Peter.' Parry tilted her head with a kindly smile and carefully released the safety catch on her weapon.

Twenty-four

I had a moment's doubt about using the ultrasonics. A village hall full of unconscious barn dancers could be difficult to explain. My hesitation only lasted for a moment, but in that moment Peter made a hurried movement towards his incapacitator and Parry sprang to her feet and levelled her own weapon at his nose. Peter's hand froze in mid-air. I took my opportunity while her attention was distracted. I fell flat on my stomach, pressed the tiny button on the ultrasonic and skimmed it across the floorboards.

Parry had obviously not expected any resistance. Her expression of astonishment was laughable as the white disc hit her in the ankle with a whumph which made the bones in my head tingle. The sensation was unnervingly pleasant. Below us, from the hall, came sounds like towers of bricks falling. The caller's voice stopped and the music of the band faded away into screeching discord. Something fell with a thump on to the roof above our heads.

I had almost been able to see the sound which knocked out everyone within a thirty metre radius.

Everyone, that was, who did not possess a Black Star earpiece. Parry kept coming. Of *course*! How could I have been so stupid? We had heard Livia saying that Parry had a Black Star communicator. I had just somehow not expected her to be wearing it now.

It was terrifying. She was a big woman. Her eyes stared in opposite directions but she kept coming straight at me. It was like being charged by a satellite tower.

'You silly boy!' She barked with laughter. 'How do you think I got here?' She patted her ear. 'With this little communicator I shall soon know everything. *Everything*, do you hear me? I just have to call your fellow conspirators one by one and I shall have them all.'

'All Black Star members! Calling all Black Star members!' It was Peter gabbling, his hand on his ear. Parry swung her incapacitor back at him but he kept on shouting. 'Do not communicate! Life and death! *Do not communicate!*'

Parry fired and Peter crumpled to the floorboards with a hollow smack. But then while the barrel was pointing away from me again I whipped out my own weapon and fired at Parry at point blank range. The alien woman swayed, sagged and fell, her outstretched arm bouncing off Peter's neck. Quickly I took out the gravity blanket from my gadgets belt and flicked it as Fenella had shown me. It dragged me forward as it enveloped Parry from the neck down. It was no more awkward than flicking a heavy duvet on to an unmade bed.

I felt rather pleased with myself. It would be a long time before she got out of that bed.

'BS Fourteen,' I called shakily. 'You can talk now.' There was silence. It was understandable caution on Fenella's part, I realised. 'OK BS Fourteen, don't speak to me then. See if I care. Listen, BS Nine is unconscious in the loft of the village hall. Two Myrions have stolen our scoot-suits so I can't get him down. Parry is here too. She's also unconscious and under a gravity blanket. She had a Black Star communicator but I'm going to take that out of her ear which should make the airwaves safe again. Livia Bunch is one of the enemy. She's here with Uncle Simon. I assume that they're unconscious too along with the rest of the local NUT. Please rescue Peter, then send a fleet of ambulances to the village hall. Take care, BS Fourteen. I'm going into hiding for the rest of this awful night. BS Eight out.'

There was no reply, but by the time I crossed the bridge over the canal I could hear sirens in the distance.

I spent the night asleep against a haystack. It was last year's hay, stored against shortages which had not occurred. It had a heavy, fermented smell and was ragged and uneven where a few bales had been taken from it to feed the cattle in winter. Other bales had fallen down and now lay in protective ramparts around me. It was warm and, I reflected, probably creeping with bugs.

I dozed, dreaming briefly. In my sleep I saw the heaped bodies in the village hall as I had seen them before I fled. Mr Rupert's expression of bliss as he lay with his head in Ms Tuttle's lap, the fiddler lying half off the platform with his bow stuck in his ear, all kept repeating themselves stupidly in my brain. But in my dream there was something much worse wrong with them than mere temporary unconsciousness. Something dreadful lurked outside. Something unspeakable and huge. A sighing shadow. The shadow of a fluorescent, black-toothed monster which reached right up to the sky.

I woke early. A cow was looking at me. I stood up stiffly and stretched. Then I went home.

Twenty-five

It was only six o'clock but Auntie was up already, sitting in the kitchen in her blue towelling dressing gown, feeding cornflakes one by one to Maureen the cat.

'Hello lad,' she said, looking pleased to have more articulate company. 'You're up early. I had such funny dreams last night. You were in them, talking to a monster.'

I laughed nervously. 'Heavens Auntie, that sounds weird. No more of that red wine for you then.' My voice rang hollow even to myself.

I helped myself to some of Maureen's cornflakes and switched on the radio, just in time to hear the end of the local news.

'. . . but the cause of the teachers' mass collapse remains a mystery,' the newscaster was saying. 'A spokeswoman for Musgrove Park Hospital in Taunton said this morning that all fifty-seven teachers and musicians are expected to leave hospital later today. Although mass hysteria has not been ruled out, further investigations are expected to take place, and experts will be travelling to Stoke Stiley village hall this morning to examine the water system and the drains.'

'Dear dear.' Auntie clicked her tongue in fascination. 'Fancy that. I always did say them teachers was a highly-strung lot. You wait till I tell your mother about this.' Mum had been a teacher once, but every time she talked about going back to it, Auntie had a fall or a dizzy turn and couldn't be left.

When I had finished my breakfast I went up to my room and lay down. I felt very tired, but there was no question of sleeping. I could not believe that the Easter holidays were nearly over. How could we ever go back to school after so much had happened – was still happening? Above all, what was I to do with Parry?

Suddenly I heard a scream outside. I sat up, tense and frightened, listening. It came again. An animal. A chair fell in the kitchen.

'Dominic!' It was Auntie's voice, panic-stricken. 'Dominic! A hawk has got your cat!' The noise outside worsened, a gurgling screech and dull fluffy fighting. I raced to the window. On the back lawn, near the far wall between the chestnut trees, a massive brown bird had Perkin in its talons and was ripping at him with its fearful curved beak. Perkin fought back, but looked helpless and small, and there was blood on his black fur. The bird looked like an eagle, I thought as I flew down the stairs. But eagles in Somerset? Ornithology strikes back.

At the back door I fumbled for the key. Auntie was clumsily picking up her walking stick. She raised it above her head and with a war cry tottered after me to the kitchen door as I flung it open. The door slammed back against the fridge leaving a mark which remains to this day. I tore Auntie's walking stick from her hands. Then I was running, down the steps, over the terrace, across the lawn.

Perkin looked dead. The gigantic bird fixed its horrid golden eye on me, then it rose effortlessly into the air with Perkin hanging from its claws like a discarded mink stole. With two beats of its wings it was over the wall.

I could hear shouts behind me now, Mum, Dad, Julia. '*Leave it, Dominic*!' screamed Mum, but I was half over the wall already, my trainers kicking dusty moss down. With a fast roll I hit the ground on the far side, and Perkin was there. He was sitting dozing among the grain. Pitch on barley. He flattened his ears and backed away as I lunged at him, gasping.

'Perkin . . .' I looked around. There was no sign of the eagle. It had vanished. The blood had vanished. Perkin looked puzzled but unhurt. I picked him up and he tucked his head under my arm just as he used to when he was a kitten.

'How touching.'

The voice was behind me, and instantly I understood everything. I did not need to see the hallucinator in Parry's outstretched hand. I knew with a slow sinking despair that the eagle had never existed.

Parry looked tired. I was pleased to see that. Two orange-uniformed guards, like those from whose grasp we had torn Mr Batworthy, stood behind her, and behind them was an orange gravity-blaster. I could hear running footsteps on the other side of our garden wall now, and with sudden hope I hurled myself at it, but it was too late. Perkin leapt on to it with a yowl, but hard hands pulled me back.

'No no, Dominic,' cooed Parry as I was tossed unceremoniously into the gravity-blaster. The three aliens piled in on top of me. We spun on the ground, in the shelter of the garden wall, flattening the barley, and had gone into hypervortex before any of my family had even reached the end of the garden path.

As we whirled, I could hear Parry's voice talking gently in my ear.

'You are our prize, Dominic dear. We have wanted another Black Star member for such a long time. Do you know it's my birthday today? I couldn't have had anything I wanted more. What a little innocent you've pretended to be. Dear me. I was quite fooled for a time. But now you're going to tell us *everything*.' She patted my cheek. We were in space now. '*All* your friends, *all* your codes, *all* your passwords . . .'

The guard who was flying the gravity-blaster flicked the controls and we surged forward. Parry settled herself in her seat and continued '. . . and then we will be able to help you. We so much want to help you, Dominic. You and all the other poor, misguided Black Star gangsters. It's for your own good. You just don't understand that yet. Then when we have removed and processed all Black Star members from the face of this dear little planet, we will be free to instil right-thinking attitudes into the rest of Earth's residents who think they are too independent to live co-operatively in a civilised universe.'

Her voice had hardened. 'Sometimes we have to be cruel to be kind, Dominic. Isn't that what you say down here? Spare the rod and spoil the child? Isn't that right, Dominic?'

As we leapt across space faster than the speed of light, I considered for the first time the possibility of failure, the possibility that Earth might be destroyed.

Twenty-six

The Alpha Centauri interchange was like a city. Perpetual daylight probes glowed overhead, surrounding us with bright, natural-looking light. Trees grew along broad avenues. Birds sang in parks.

'We find that natural conditions are essential to people's mental health in space,' Parry explained, clearly unaware of any irony, as we walked from the space terminal and along a wide street. The two Council guards walked one on either side of me, their hands never relaxing their grip on my arms.

A glass-windowed skyscraper confronted us at the end of the avenue. Automatic doors opened as we approached it. Inside, at a reception desk, Parry touched her hand to a glass screen. A purple light flashed.

'Pass,' said the man at the desk.

'This prisoner is for interrogation and processing.' Parry indicated that I should put my right hand to the screen. There seemed little point in arguing, so I did. An orange light flashed. 'We just have to wait now while the entry computer processes your purple pass. How do you feel, Dominic? There's no need to be afraid.' She sat down on a nearby plastic chair and gestured to me to do the same.

'I feel extremely bad,' I replied shortly. Parry smiled and shook her head.

'My dear boy, you mustn't.' She patted my shoulder. 'Do you think I don't know that you've been led into this? We have our suspicions as to who is responsible, and in due course they will be helped to see things differently too. Surely you can't wish to defend a world system which depends on mutual aggression?'

I was silent for a moment. Was there any point in entering into a discussion with Parry? Was there even the remotest hope that she might listen to my point of view? I spoke slowly and cautiously.

'Parry . . . is it all right if I call you Parry?' I treated myself to a mental picture of Fenella's and Peter's satirical laughter at this. Who was sweet-talking the enemy now?

Parry tucked her chin in and gave me a benign, crinkle-eyed smile. 'Dominic dear, you just go on calling me Parry. We'll leave it to the less intelligent to call me Commander.'

I swallowed.

'Well, Parry . . . you see . . . er . . . sometimes it's better to let people work things out for themselves. Don't you agree? You know, if you impose a system on people, they have a natural resistance to it. If they come to the right conclusions themselves, perhaps because they've been set a good example, then they're more likely to stick to them.' I wished she would stop patting my shoulder but I decided to bear it for a while longer.

Parry laughed merrily. She rocked in her chair.

'Oh my dear boy, and what happens in the mean-time? They just carry on threatening each other? They develop their fusion bombs and blow us all sky high? When we could allow them the benefits of our own hard-earned experience? And who's to say they would ever come to the right conclusions anyway? No no Dominic. There is a quick way to make all you Earth people hate and fear your new fusion bombs as much as we do in our more advanced civilisations, and to make your planet too chaotic for anyone to think about travelling into outer space for a while. A quick way, a simple way, two little demonstrations, one in the East and one in the West, of what happens when the bombs are detonated. And you'll be doing it to yourselves. It won't be us letting the bombs off . . .'

I felt sick, but fought for words, for the right combinations of sound and structure which could perhaps change her mind.

'But it's only . . . only because you've interfered with the brains of our world leaders, Parry. They wouldn't be doing this otherwise. It's really you who are the aggressors, which is what you say you disapprove of.'

Parry guffawed. 'Oh dear, you are quick aren't you Dominic.'

I sat forward, partly to get away from her patting hand and partly to assess my chances of escaping. I wanted to ask her about Mr Batworthy but did not dare risk being forced to reveal where he was. The glass screen flashed with purple light and Parry rose to her feet. The two guards seized my arms again and hauled me upright. Parry gave me a bright smile, patted her hair, now that she was deprived of my shoulder, then turned and strode on ahead.

'Cruel to be kind,' she repeated, glancing back as the two guards dragged me along behind them. I shook angrily at their imprisoning hands.

'Do you always talk in clichés?' I shouted.

Parry sighed. 'Take him first to the search room, guards. Unlike the last three, this one is *not* going to get away. Follow me.'

An escalator took us up several floors and then turned into moving corridors, one to the left and one to the right. We stepped on to the left-hand one. The few people using the corridors stared at us.

'You're brainwashed, all of you!' I shouted. 'You're zombies! Don't you want to be free, and think for yourselves?' There were a few smiles and titters.

Having the floor moving rapidly beneath my feet was unnerving – like Heathrow but five times faster. I staggered and would have fallen if the guards had not been holding me up. Suddenly, ahead, I saw that we were approaching the outer wall of the skyscraper. In it, an open doorway gaped out on to empty air. I stared at it in horrified disbelief. There was nothing to stop us. The moving corridor was zooming relentlessly towards a fifteen storey drop. I gave a yelp of sheer terror and tried to turn and run, but the guards held on to me, sniggering.

This was it then. So much for talk of processing and helping. They were going to tip me out of a skyscraper into oblivion. I could see now that the moving floor of the corridor turned back on itself at the opening like a conveyor belt, so any faint hopes I might have had of an invisible corner at the end, faded. I gave a sudden mighty wrench and broke free of the guards. I had run the wrong way up escalators before, and I could run the wrong way along this moving corridor now. With flailing arms I thrust Parry aside and began to run. One of the guards put out his foot and tripped me. With a rib-cracking thump I sprawled full length.

'Calm *down*, Dominic,' I heard Parry shouting in exasperation. 'It's only . . .' But by now I had managed to get my hand into my gadgets belt. I found the cold metal of the copper bracelet, thrust my hand into it and jumped to my feet.

Someone screamed behind me. The guards stepped back, chalk white. To myself I looked normal, but I knew what I must look like to them. I remembered all too clearly the fluorescent monster with black teeth which had confronted me in the shed. I straightened up to my full height, nearly at the edge now, and bared my teeth.

'Get him!' shrieked Parry. 'It's only a trick! A Black Star trick! There's no monster here!' It did cross my mind at this stage to wonder why no one else seemed unduly worried about approaching the edge of the precipice. I started to move backwards, raising my arms and growling. Even Parry blanched. She was only two metres from the opening now. Then she was over it.

She did not fall. She flew. She was catapulted across an invisible bridge, and landed in an identical doorway in the skyscraper opposite.

I stood and gaped. Then the guards were over too, soaring in a massive bound to land where Parry had landed, high in the opposite building. Seconds later, having stood still in astonishment for too long, I followed them.

It was like flying without wings. I could feel the invisible force field gripping me by the hips and feet and whirling me through the air, then I landed, with my knees buckling, in a moving corridor on the other side.

This corridor, a two-directional one, was full, but not for long. I snarled and roared and waved my arms at the crowd of people who were coming towards me.

'Good God, what is it?' a six foot blonde in green pyjamas whispered. Then the crowd started to scream and run. I chased them. I hooked my fingers and lunged at them. I had a sudden mental time-warp of playing chasing games in the playground. For a moment it was hard to realise that this was for real. People staggered and started running on the spot as they tried to escape down the wrong side of the corridor and the moving floor overtook them.

Then the corridor curved around to the left, and Parry and the guards were waiting for me, their incapacitators raised. They fired at close range. As I hit the floor a blur of thoughts flickered across my mind. One in the East and one in the West. All those people dead. All that grief and agony.

I was also terribly afraid that that the aliens had not done their homework. They did not know us well enough. The conflict would hardly stop with just two bombs. And hadn't they heard of the killing, dust-laden skies of nuclear winter? As I lost consciousness I knew that the end of life on Earth was staring me in the face, and I was powerless to stop it.

Twenty-seven

I felt as though I had slept for a long time. My first awareness was of a pounding headache. My limbs were heavy and slow and my mind fuddled. I awoke sluggishly to find myself lying on a strange, diagonally sloping bed in a room with white walls. Something sticky was attached to my forehead. It wrinkled my skin as I opened my eyes. I could hear a low, male voice behind me, speaking the interplanetary language. At least, I realised with surprise, my memory did not seem to have been impaired so far.

'No, you're quite right,' said the voice. 'Your memory hasn't been erased yet.' I jerked my head round in shock. I had not spoken, but the voice had answered my thought. It continued. 'In fact you haven't been through the computers at all yet. That comes next. So far we have simply been taking all sorts of useful information out of your brain. No point in wiping everything out until we've had what we need, is there? Here, see this screen? Oh, you can't turn round can you. Maybe it's just as well because whatever you think simply appears on it.'

I felt myself go cold. My limbs started trembling.

'What . . . ?' I asked with difficulty. 'What have I said?'

The owner of the voice appeared. He was a young man of about twenty-five with short, fair hair and a benevolent smile.

'Said? Nothing, old son. Not a word. We printed it all out straight from your brain.' He waved a piece of paper at me. 'The fair Fenella's name never passed your lips.' He turned away, laughing, and resumed his conversation with the other, unseen, person behind me.

'So what have the powers-that-be decided? Unit Three takes Fenella Brown? Unit Four takes Mitzalie Rasper?'

'Yes. Then Unit Ten takes the Baxendale boy and Unit Twenty-five takes Claude Rasper.' It was a woman's voice. The man laughed again.

'God, that was a surprise! I thought old Parry was going to have a heart attack when his name came up. She used to fancy him, you know.'

I looked down at myself. I was wearing a smooth, white, hospital-type robe. My arms were strapped to the bed. There was no comforting weight of my Black Star gadgets belt and I had no doubt, too, that the Black Star communicator would be gone from my ear. My head throbbed painfully. Uninvited, a tear bulged out of my left eye and ran down into my ear. So this was how it was ending. It was all over for me, all over for the Black Star Gang, and worse still, all over for Earth, because now there would be no one left to prevent the lesson which the United Council intended to teach us.

'I want to speak to Parry!' I called out. My throat felt dry. The young man came back and deftly detached the sticky disc which had robbed my brain of its secrets. The small hairs at the edge of my hairline pulled painfully as the adhesive peeled off.

'You can't. She's having a nervous breakdown. She's applied for double processing and a week's leave.' I could hear both him and the woman chuckling. 'Anyway, it's time to wheel you down to the computer room. We had some lovely new brain processors delivered by the Dupronic. You'll like them. They make you feel *really* good. Do you want me to program you a little extra euphoria to see you through the next few days? It's really no trouble.'

I glared at him and shook my head. 'I must speak to Parry. Is it true that they're going to drop bombs on Earth?'

The young man leaned close. I saw that his name tag said Resbibie. He put on a mock-sad face and clicked his tongue reproachfully. I hated him more every minute. He spoke in confidential tones.

'My dear, er . . .' He glanced at the sheet of paper in his hand. '. . . Dominic. You obviously haven't got the message at *all* about our peaceful universe. We don't drop bombs. We're going to let you lot down there drop one of yours. Then the other side will retaliate. I understand that a situation of extreme political tension is arising at this very moment. I daresay you could ask to stay up here until it's all over.'

Briskly he started to push my imprisoning bed along. I had not realised until now that it was on wheels.

'Oh no.' I must have moaned out loud, because he patted my arm. I shrugged him away and struggled in my smooth, slippery gown, but with my arms fastened down all I could do was slither about inside it.

We launched ourselves into the air between the two buildings at the invisible crossing, heading for a different entrance from the one which had so terrified me the first time. All the way up and down the street I could see other people flying to and fro between the buildings.

'Hey look!' My escort suddenly let go of one side of my trolley and pointed. I tipped horrifyingly to one side, but between trying to swivel my body back and keep my balance, I did as he said, and looked. In the sky, at the far end of the broad street, four massive orange gravity-blasters hung motionless. Then, as I watched, slowly they began to revolve.

'They're going to get your friends,' Resbibie told me as we landed in the opposite doorway with a jolt that nearly dislocated my hip. The moving corridor swept us along. 'What an inspiring sight,' my captor burbled on. 'We must all be very pleased and thankful for your friends, mustn't we? They will feel so much better when their abnormal tendencies are eradicated and they are able to be useful and conforming members of society again.'

'You're a self-righteous moron,' I remarked tiredly. 'You have less sense than my aunt's cat.' I closed my eyes.

'Dear me.' Resbibie gave my trolley a brisk shove. 'Is that a quaint Earth saying or something? You poor misguided boy. Never mind, we'll soon have you right.

140

Hadzander is on duty in the computer room today. You should be honoured. He's head of the department. Unfortunately he's sometimes a little over-conscientious, but I don't believe all that stuff I hear about people being permanently brain-damaged by the time they come out. It's too bad that his appearance is so intimidating. He can't help that of course. I certainly don't believe that people have died of fright just from looking at him. Anyway you can look forward to not having any subversive leanings after he's finished with you.'

'It seems to me that you should be brain-processed against petty spitefulness,' I said nastily. I felt briefly happy at the strange liberty of insulting these clockwork authority figures.

But my happiness was to be short-lived. At a T-junction in the long corridor we turned left and stepped off the moving belt into a short, red-painted hall. At the end of it double glass doors opened before us. Revealed inside the room were familiar banks of computers with their coffin-like drawers. People were queueing up in orderly rows between chrome railings as if they were at the post office. Many turned and smiled dutifully at our entrance. A few eyebrows were raised at my diagonal advent on wheels.

'Black Star member,' announced my captor smugly to all and sundry. Jaws dropped and eyes bulged. Dozens of avid gazes swung on to me then away again with furtive politeness, as though I were a chimpanzee in one of those old twentieth-century zoos, doing something interesting but unmentionable.

'You are all puppets!' I yelled. 'You let them interfere with your brains! Stop them! Can't you see what they're doing to you?'

There were embarrassed grins. It was then that I first heard the voice.

'What's all this?' it enquired. It sounded like a yeti or a caveman, ice-cold but with a primitive brutality and inhumanity behind it like nothing I had ever heard before. A door clicked shut and footsteps approached, out of sight behind me. Other people turned to look, and foolish ingratiating smiles spread across faces.

'It's Hadzander, the chief programmer,' whispered Resbibie. He raised his voice. 'I have the Black Star member, sir. He's creating a disturbance.' He turned my trolley so that I could face the Voice. All last vestiges of hope left me in that moment. Hadzander looked like anthropomorphized evil.

He had a thin, long, concave face, the sort that small children draw for witches, and an expression of such malignancy that cold sweat broke out all over my body.

'Oh no.' I could not tell whether I had said it or merely thought it. Not that it made much difference round here anyway.

The deep V of the man's eyebrows exactly paralleled the eroded scowling grooves in his forehead. Straight black and grey hair grew sharply back from his brow. He was of medium height, but stooping, which made him appear shorter and more ancient. As he leaned close to me I saw that coarse open pores surrounded his lips and nose.

'So this is Dominic.' There was silence in the rest of

the room. This man did not need to pretend to forget one's name. I stared at the hairs growing out of his nose. He went on. 'I am Hadzander, Dominic, and I am here to help you. However I am afraid it may not be easy. You are clearly a very bad boy.'

There were gasps. Shock horror! Here was someone actually being accused of being bad, not just misguided or ignorant. I tried to speak but my voice had seized up in my throat. Hadzander turned to my escort.

'As you can see, Resbibie, we have queues. The end of the month is always busy and we cannot keep responsible citizens waiting because of the likes of him. Also, I have to work out a special program for this ... renegade. I don't want to destroy too many of his brain cells, but we can't risk leaving any wilfulness or aggression at all in someone like this. Take him into the red anteroom for now and I will interview him personally.'

I heard a sob from someone in one of the queues. A look of malicious satisfaction crossed Resbibie's face and he swung me round again and propelled me towards a red door on the far side of the room, where the computers ended. Hadzander walked beside us with lithe, mincing steps, at odds with his posture. It was the walk of a torturer, or of a panther stalking its prey. He held the red door open for the trolley to pass through.

Inside, the anteroom was small with white walls, red armchairs and a red plastic coffee table. The chief programmer steadied the trolley as Resbibie bumped me down a step and up a thick-pile red rug.

'Release his arms.' He made a peremptory gesture. Resbibie dithered uncertainly.

'He's very violent, sir.'

'Tut tut.' Hadzander loomed over me and peered into my eyes with infinite disdain. A pleased smile spread across his bony face. 'No matter. I love a challenge. Release his hands, lad. Do you think he will dare to harm me? Look at him. He trembles like a jellyfish.'

Resbibie did as he was bidden. I could feel Hadzander's breath on my face as he bent closer. The skin below his eyes was mud-grey. He flapped an arm behind him.

'All right, lad. Go back to your duties. I have to . . . *question* this misguided child.' What I can only describe as an anticipatory leer distorted his features. I heard a quick shuffle as Resbibie left, his relief almost palpable in the air. The door clicked and I wished with all my heart that he had stayed.

Suddenly the chief programmer frowned. My heart gave a violent jolt. I felt he must be about to kill me. He stroked his chin and stared at me with a narrow-eyed tilt of his head. 'That's odd,' he muttered softly. 'Didn't we meet aboard the Starship Ashkey?'

Twenty-eight

I was in a maintenance shaft, waiting. Waiting for the voices above me to stop. I was standing in a small lift, a claustrophobic cage.

My mind was still racing from the shock of Hadzander's revelation. Belief had been long moments in coming. After the first heart-stopping passwords, I had realised that he might be trying to trick me. My interrogators could easily have picked the passwords from my brain prints. It was only when I saw the black star on the chief programmer's palm, that I believed. He had laughed at me, but had quickly become serious.

'Dominic, there may still be time to save Black Star members on Earth, but frankly it's going to be up to you. We can't set up anyone else fast enough. As for Earth itself, well BS One is desperately trying to sabotage the Council's plans, but I don't hold out much hope. Try and get Fenella, Mitzalie, Claude and Peter into deep space at these co-ordinates.' He scribbled some numbers on my palm. 'We will then come for you if there are any of us left.'

The same clawlike hand that had scribbled the

numbers, prised the maintenance grille from the wall with a small crowbar and helped me through the gap. The cagelike lift hung waiting.

'I pulled it up to this floor when I heard they were bringing you in. Go up one floor. Here's the up and down lever. There are ultrasonics under the first floor panel of the room you come to. Use one there. That will also deal with people on this floor and the roof. Then go down through the building using one at each alternate floor. The gravity-blaster hangars are at ground level, sixteen storeys down. Get back to Earth fast, and . . .' he hesitated '. . . don't go near Bristol.'

He saw my shocked look. 'Yes.' He seemed to be lost for words for a moment. 'Yes, it's to be Bristol and St Petersburg.' He pulled himself together and continued. 'Here's my Black Star communicator. It's only useful as protection from the ultrasonics now, until we have a new secret wavelength. Now hit me with this.' He handed me the small crowbar.

I took it and trembled.

'I can't. I might kill you.'

'*Do* it. Not *too* hard for heaven's sake. Just enough to draw blood. It's for my own protection. I can't afford to arouse suspicion. There's no way the entire Black Star Gang can avoid their monthly brainwashing without me in one piece.'

He suddenly gripped me painfully by the arm. 'Dominic, I love computers. But one day you and I will destroy these evil machines. We will find the central control and eliminate it. Then when people's minds are free, we will build new computers which will be our

146

servants, not our masters, like your primitive little machines down there on Earth.'

Voices sounded outside.

'Better not interrupt. He's interrogating a Black Star member.'

'But it's urgent.'

'Is anything *that* urgent?'

'Hm, well . . .'

The voices faded, but I knew our time was running out. Carefully, I hit him.

Now, hanging poised in the darkness between two floors, I listened to the voices in the room where the ultrasonics were hidden. Surely whoever was there must go soon. Clearly Hadzander had not anticipated that the room might be in use. I had hung there for several minutes by the time the voices stopped, then I heard the click and swish of a door. How long, I wondered, before someone would dare to interrupt Hadzander in the red anteroom and find him lying on the floor feigning unconsciousness, a bruise rapidly colouring his forehead. I hoped it was convincing.

When they did discover him, then I would have no time left. They would know that there was only one way I could have gone.

I waited for a few more seconds, then ascended to the next grille. The room was empty. It was some sort of conference room, with a long metal table and a dozen shiny metal chairs. Cautiously I dislodged the grille, holding it through the bars to prevent it from falling to the floor, but unable to avoid a loud metallic clang as it sprang loose.

The first floor panel, he had said. The floor was laid in long black polished strips. Carefully I stepped down into the room. The first floor panel tilted slightly under my foot. Without difficulty I levered it up and stood it on its side against a chairleg. A gadgets belt lay flat in the space underneath. Pinned to it was a note on a piece of lined scrap paper. It said, 'Rather you than me, friend. Good luck. I hope I'm not in the building when these things go off. BS One.'

I smiled, suddenly filled with irrational hope. It faded fast. There was no time to spare.

I strapped the belt over my absurd white robe and climbed back into the cage lift. It was awkward to refit the grille from the inside, and I wasted precious moments. Then, with utmost care, I took out one of the ultrasonics. The priming button was on the concave side. I held it against the grille. Yes, it would fit between the bars. I primed it and dropped it through.

Ultrasonics make the bones in your head vibrate like a tuning fork, and this includes your sinuses, even with the protection of a Black Star communicator in your ear. Consequently my nose was running by the time I reached the next floor down. Apprehensively I stopped the lift and peered through the grille. Hadzander lay where I had left him, but no longer alone. The red door stood open, and two Council guards and a woman in cream pyjamas lay sprawled across the threshold. By craning my neck I could just see a corner of the computer room through the open door. The queues had gone down like dominoes.

By the time I reached the next floor down there was

shouting and running going on. I soon put a stop to that. Sixteen storeys is a long way though. Might word travel faster than this lift?

It did.

The grille was already off and an incapacitator pointing through the opening as I descended, feet first, to ground floor level. With the gentlest touch of my thumb I primed my last ultrasonic and held it while it activated. It nearly blew my hair off.

Twenty-nine

A lot of gravity-blasters stood in the space hangar. Bodies lay around, but no one moved. They would stay like that for at least an hour, according to what Fenella had told me. Fenella. My chest tightened painfully. Had they captured her and the others yet? Would my friends understand that the information had been extracted from me without my knowledge?

I climbed out of the shaft with cramp in my legs, my nose streaming and a feeling of being slightly high. I wiped my nose on my flowing white sleeve. My eyes ranged along the gravity-blasters in the hangar and I chose a small black shiny vehicle with electric blue flashes along the sides. It might be fast. Its design suggested ownership by a speed fanatic and its controls looked similar to those I had operated before. The space doors of the hangar stood open. There was nothing in my way.

I was about to climb into the little vehicle when a faint humming came to my ears. I froze and looked around me. I could see nothing which would account for the humming. Then I realised as the noise grew louder that it was coming from outside the space doors. A moment later I saw it, a yellow gravity-blaster homing in fast towards the Alpha Centauri Interchange. It was approaching too quickly for me to escape before it arrived.

I leapt back into the shadows which edged the hangar, almost tripping over a Council guard who had fallen with his hand outstretched towards a large control box. The control box afforded me some shelter, but I knew I had only moments before the newcomers realised that there were bodies sprawled all over the hangar. I had used my last ultrasonic. I was unprotected. I flattened myself against the concrete wall in the shadow of the control box, and waited.

'Gravity and air' said a notice on the control box in the hieroglyphics of the interplanetary language. I tried to minimise my breathing as the yellow gravity-blaster docked and two men in white space suits got out.

'Blasted radiation regulators,' said one. 'They've never been the same since they started making them out of bioplastic. I'd like to see the blasted designers hanging upside down in blasted space trying to fix the blasted things.' He took off his helmet and saw the first body. He jerked to a halt. 'Nideus! Look over here!' He stooped to where an orange-suited guard lay outstretched in the shadow of a mooring bay. The other man took off his helmet and joined him. Next to the guard lay his incapacitator. How I wished that I had picked it up as I ran for cover.

They were puzzled. One of them felt the guard's pulse and heart.

'He's out like a light, but his breathing's OK. We'd better get him up to the hospital. Must have fallen and bashed his head.'

But the other man touched his companion's arm and silently shook his head, glancing around the hangar nervously.

'Sh. No. There's something odd here.' His voice was barely audible. 'It's been ten minutes since we could make contact by communicator. Maybe it *wasn't* just interference from the radiation regulators.'

The two men straightened up slowly, back to back, and peered around them. Nideus bent watchfully and picked up the guard's incapacitator. My heart sank. Another guard lay close to where I was hiding. His leg stuck out from the shadows. It could only be moments before they saw him. What could I use to protect myself? There must be something. I couldn't be recaptured now. My eyes returned to the control box labelled 'Gravity and air'. Slowly and with the utmost caution I tried its plastic door. It was locked. Surreptitiously I transferred the maintenance shaft crowbar, which I still held, from my left hand to my right.

Then they saw him.

'Bridon, there's another one.' Nideus's voice was quiet as he pointed.

'Sh. Careful.'

The two repair men crept in my direction and crouched by the second guard. Bridon's hand was only a metre from my foot, but still they did not see me. They checked him as they had the first guard. I felt a strange kinship with them. They were like me, just ordinary people. Only brainwashed. The simple basic freedom of thinking their own thoughts had been taken from them. Yet, like farmed animals, they did not appear to mind. Was all this really worth the effort, my tired mind wondered subversively? Was freedom of thought such a precious commodity as all that? The answer came back to me immediately. Yes.

Bridon had raised his head from the guard. 'He's all right, only blasted unconscious.' Suddenly he looked down again at the unconscious man. 'Oh no . . .' he whispered, peering more closely. He uttered a couple of interesting swear words I had never heard before.

'What? What is it?'

'Look. Look at the expression on his face. Look at that silly smile. He looks too happy by half. Come to think of it, the other one did too. You know what leaves people like this, don't you, Nideus. Don't you remember? It's those things the Black Star Gang uses . . .'

They straightened up sharply, then Bridon saw me. He let out a yell. I was sorry that they should be so frightened of me, that they should genuinely see me as a dangerous alien. If it had been he and not Nideus who had the incapacitator in his hand things could have turned out very differently. As it was, I had the thin end of the crowbar already pushed behind the control box door, and with a savage jerk of my wrist I levered it open, smashing plastic and wood into splinters. A follow-through reflex slammed down the gravity lever to its full extent, way past settings which said 'Normal' and 'Extra', right into the 'Danger' zone.

We all fell to the floor. It was a terrifying sensation,

but unlike the others I was prepared for it. I crawled and dragged myself across the floor, glued to the ground as though in one of those immobilising dreams where your legs are trapped by sleep and the bedclothes, and the monster is after you.

Panting, dripping with sweat, I reached the black gravity-blaster. Would it take off in this excessive gravity? It had to. I dared not look behind me. I hauled legs which seemed to weigh a tonne each, one by one over the rim and into the cabin of the vehicle. Then I fell in after them. My arms were like lead weights as I lifted them to the controls. The glass dome juddered shut, then I nearly went through it as normal gravity came on inside the cabin. I could look outside now. The two repair men were still struggling to stand. Nideus began to half-crawl towards the control box. The gravity-blaster wobbled and shook, but did not rise from its bay as I operated the controls. I opened it up to full power. Normally this would have taken me straight through the ceiling, but now it just managed to raise me on a thin cushion of air, like a hovercraft, a few centimetres above the ground. Lopsidedly we waltzed towards the exit doors. I willed the machine forward, my hands jammed on the controls. One side scraped the concrete floor. I moved in my seat to even out the weight. Then we were out.

Whether it was the lightness of space or whether Nideus reached the control box in that moment I shall never know, but the gravity-blaster shot forward with such force that I was wrenched from my seat at its controls and slammed backwards into the storage cupboards. The renewed headache it gave me was almost a pleasure.

For once, space failed to impress. My mind was racing as I switched on the computer's voice control.

'Co-ordinates for Stoke Stiley, Somerset, Planet Earth please,' I said to it distractedly.

'62 555 01. Who are you anyway?'

Oh dear. Who needed an inquisitive computer just now?

'Just a wanted outlaw,' I replied as I keyed in the co-ordinates. The computer gave a startled hiccup and was silent.

I thought back to my conversation with Hadzander. He had said that the Black Star communicator which he gave me was useful only as protection from ultrasonics until a new secret wavelength was developed, but I wondered. What did I have to lose? The Council's agents already knew my voice and identity. If I called Fenella and the others as soon as I came within transmitting range of Earth, might I conceivably be in time to warn them of their danger? How long ago had the huge Council gravity-blasters left? So much had happened it seemed like a week, but it could be as little as an hour. They might only just be approaching Earth's atmosphere at this moment.

Twenty minutes later Earth was visible on my screen, blue and green, cloudy and beautiful, a flawed jewel. It was still far distant, but maybe near enough for some sort of communication.

I pulled my left earlobe. I had still seen no sign of the

Council gravity-blasters. Perhaps I was too late after all. What I didn't want to see was them heading back.

'BS Eight calling BS Fourteen, BS Nine, BS Thirty and BS Twenty. BS Eight calling . . .'

An astonished, distorted whisper came into my ear.

'BS Eight, this is BS Twenty. Where are you?' It was Claude, his voice faint and crackly.

'Approaching the solar system. Are you all right?'

'Yes. Of course. What's happening?'

'The Council captured me. There's no time to explain. They're coming for all of you too. They know that you, Fenella, Mitzalie and Peter are Black Star members. There's no point in concealing names any more. You have to get away *now*. Council soldiers are on their way to capture you, and they must be almost there by now . . .'

His horrified voice interrupted me.

'They're here. It's too late.'

'Go! Go!' I screamed, but there was no reply, just a faint crackling across space.

Thirty

It was late afternoon when I arrived home, almost tea time, time to put the kettle on and raid the cake tin. The whole concept was like something from a lost life.

No one was in except Julia. She eyed my white robe with disbelief and rolled her eyes in dismay.

'Brother dear, where have you *been*? Dad's furious. Why did you run off like that after the eagle got Perkin? I said to Dad it was probably because you were so upset.'

'Run off?' I sat weakly down in a chair in the living room. 'Is that what you all think? That I ran off?'

Julia frowned and nodded. 'What else is there to think?'

What else indeed?

'Yes, I was, er, upset. I'm just going upstairs to change.'

Julia pulled at my robe. 'Why are you wearing a nightie, Dominic?'

I turned exhaustedly towards the stairs. 'I was captured by aliens.' I glanced back at her over my shoulder.

'Oh very funny. Well I suggest you think of a better story than that before Mum and Dad get home.'

I heard a car in the drive and ran upstairs.

My corpse-in-the-cupboard escapade was nothing compared with the trouble I was in this time. I had never seen Dad so angry. He was shaking with rage. It was surprisingly alarming. He accused me of worrying my mother half to death. Auntie began to sob in a corner, her image of harmless Humphrey obviously shattered beyond repair. Then I was banished to my room without any tea, as if I were six. I hardly cared. I could not have eaten anyway.

There seemed no point in trying any further to contact my friends, as I had been doing continuously and unsuccessfully since I entered Earth's atmosphere, but I did try just once more. The airwaves were empty.

I wondered what had happened to Mr Batworthy up there on Claude's farm. When all the family were safely eating dinner I rang Directory Enquiries for Claude's viewphone number and tried ringing the farm. There was no reply.

Later I risked coming downstairs to watch the Nine O'Clock News on television. Unsmilingly my mother presented me with a bowl of Coco Pops and milk. I thanked her and sat down.

'Here is the Nine O'Clock News with Felicity Shackleton.' The amazingly beautiful newscaster had dark hair and large blue eyes and reminded me of Fenella.

'The international crisis deepened today with . . .'

My hair stood on end. It was happening. It was really happening. I was so tired that I had almost stopped believing it for a few hours. I jumped to my feet, spilling my cereal.

'. . . and after withdrawing from the talks President Chestikov said that he found Britain's intervention in his nation's affairs quite incomprehensible. The Russian newspaper *Communism Reborn* today carried denunciations of British actions in support of the Free Russian Rebels, and called them highly provocative.

'Lady Thatcher, who will be a hundred and five later this year, made a speech in the House of Lords outlining the ways in which she feels the government could have handled the crisis better . . .'

'Dominic, what a mess.' Mum flapped her hand at my spilt cereal. 'Get a cloth from the kitchen.'

But I put my bowl shakily down on the coffee table.

'Mum, Dad, there's going to be a war . . .'

They stared at me. Dad's expression softened slightly.

'I know it looks bad, Dominic, but I doubt it will come to war. We've been saying this on and off ever since the Communist coup put paid to democracy in Russia again, but it never does seem to come to war.'

'People were starving, you see,' put in Auntie, who had always been rather left-wing, 'They wanted the old ways back. Forty years of freedom and they were still starving. You can't eat freedom.'

We all stared at her in surprise. She shrugged. Suddenly I was overwhelmed with how much I loved them all. Could I save them? Where could we go if I crammed them all into the black gravity-blaster and took off into deep space? I had the co-ordinates that Hadzander had given me still legible on my palm, but how could any of my family survive as outlaws on the run in a completely alien environment? No, they would be better off taking their chances on Earth, and I would stay with them.

What I could do was try and speak to the politicians and newspapers. I would probably end up in the care of the school psychologist at the first mention of aliens from outer space, but I could try.

At that moment the doorbell rang. My first instinct was to go and hide in the wardrobe. I began to understand the Myrions' liking for cupboards. Dad went to answer it.

'Is Dominic in? I know it's rather late ...' It was Peter. I raced into the hall and we confronted each other, wild-eyed and temporarily speechless. Peter looked exhausted. His hair was back to its normal colour now, but was dirty and untidy. The last time I had seen him he had been senseless in the loft of the village hall.

'Come upstairs,' I said.

'Don't be too late,' said Mum, heading for the kitchen. 'Don't forget school starts again on Wednesday. You ought to get back to normal bedtimes. Anyway I think the sooner we put this day behind us the better.'

'Yes Mum.'

We went up to my room. Peter collapsed on the bed and lay with one foot hanging on to the floor.

160

'What happened?' I asked.

'First things first,' he said bleakly. 'As far as my parents are concerned I've been with you all day, OK? We went along the river to Langport.'

I felt this was the least of our worries. I nodded. 'Yes. Go on.'

'Well to go back to when I last saw you, Fenella got me out of the loft and brought me home by gravity-blaster, then she went back to deal with Parry. The rest you probably know. Parry had gone, presumably rescued by Council soldiers. Your warning today came just in time. Claude managed to escape in his gravity-blaster and came for Fenella and Mitzalie just one step ahead of the Council soldiers. He came for me too, but I wouldn't go with them.'

'Good grief, why ever not, Peter?'

Peter paused. His eyes had a strange glitter to them. 'Partly because I could never have come back. Their departure was very final, I'm afraid, and I don't want to leave Earth. But more because there may be something I . . . we . . . can do to stop what is happening. You see, Council soldiers came for me after that. They've been holding me in one of their gravity-blasters orbiting Earth ever since. They told me what's going to happen. It's as you thought. They've interfered with the brains of some of the top world leaders and programmed them to overreact to each other's actions and start a war. A war using . . .'

'. . . the new fusion bombs.' I finished the sentence for him.

'You know.'

'Yes. Parry enjoyed telling me.'

'So anyway they took my communicator, then a message came through to them from their headquarters, and they simply brought me back down here and let me go. I've only just arrived. They put me down in the field at the back of your garden.'

'Why did they let you go?'

Peter rubbed his hand across his face. I peered at him, unsure whether it was dirt or tears that streaked his cheeks.

'They said it was the worst punishment they could think of.'

We were silent for a few moments.

'And have they gone?' I asked finally.

Peter nodded. 'Yes, all of them. They said they've set up what had to be set up. Whole fleets of gravity-blasters are heading back out to Alpha Centauri. There were obviously thousands of them down here. They're leaving it to us. They say they'll be back when they feel we've learnt our lesson . . . and when the fallout has cleared.'

I struggled with the concept that this was reality. That the world was going to war.

'There must be something we can do. I know! Suppose we were to show the prime minister one of the gravity-blasters! They might believe us then. They might realise that people who can build something like that could tamper with their minds as well.'

'Yes, that's a good idea. The newspapers too. That might be even better.'

We stared at each other and hope flickered.

'It'll have to be tomorrow.' Peter rubbed his eyes again in a gesture of exhaustion. 'Nobody will agree to see us tonight. I'll come round at five tomorrow morning and we'll start phoning.'

I nodded. Peter turned to go but I put out my hand to stop him.

'Peter, supposing . . . there's no tomorrow?'

He shook his head, and I realised he was probably right. The crisis was worsening fast but had not yet reached flashpoint. Perhaps there was time.

Thirty-one

I let myself out of the house by the back door in the early morning. It was still dark over the village but pale light was leaking into the sky beyond the back hedge. I had left the black gravity-blaster in the shadow of the collapsed haystack and had covered it over with fallen bales of hay. I could see before I was halfway across the field that it had gone. In desperation I pulled the haystack to pieces, searching, then I hunted along the waking hedgerows and by the canal. Finally I trudged up to the back wall of the Old Rectory. Might there be a slim possibility that the aliens had overlooked Fenella's gravity-blaster in their hasty removal of everything that was theirs?

I swung myself once more over the crumbling red brick wall. The shed door stood open. The shed was empty.

Slowly I made my way home, pulling the communicator given to me by Hadzander from my ear as I walked. It was just a useless sliver of metal now. Even so, after a few moments, I put it back again.

'Hello,' I said, pulling my left earlobe. There was no reply.

We tried, despite our lack of evidence, to interest someone in our story. We rang our MP. He declined to give us the viewphone number for Downing Street but assured us he personally would tell the prime minister how concerned modern youngsters were about peace. At the mention of aliens he laughed and said that was a matter for the Immigration Office. We rang the newspapers. They mostly suggested that we should contact the UFO Society. We rang all ten television stations and their suggestions ranged from 'Hm, very interesting but why don't you write it all down and send us a letter together with some concrete evidence of this alien invasion' to 'Hang on a moment and I'll put you through to the drama producer.'

By evening, we had given up, and next morning we went back to school.

School was utterly bizarre. Peter and I sat in class unable to concentrate. Fenella had gone. Ms Bunch had gone. Mr Batworthy had gone and so had three more teachers. Remaining staff members grumbled at having to cover for them, clearly mystified at the reasons for the exodus.

'How rude of the Browns to leave without saying goodbye,' Mum had said indignantly at breakfast that morning. On the early local radio news it was reported that a young policewoman had gone missing on duty in Somerset and that extensive searches were being made.

By lunchtime I was very thankful that the new term

had begun on a Wednesday. I doubted whether I could have survived a whole week.

Homework was piled on. Everyone else seemed rested and energetic after their holiday, but as the days went by Peter and I could neither work nor sleep. Our classwork was careless and our homework almost non-existent.

On Friday afternoon my form teacher, Mr McLiffy, took me to one side and asked me if I was ill, or if something was bothering me.

I shook my head. For a brief moment I allowed the idea of confiding everything to Mr McLiffy, of telling him that the world was on the brink of extermination, to flit through my mind. Then I came back to reality. Even empathetic English teachers have their limits of belief.

The crisis was very bad by Friday night. A newsflash during 'The Flintstones' announced that Russian Embassy staff had been recalled to Moscow from Washington and London. I went to bed and lay awake until the early hours thinking about life (if any) after the bomb.

If the scientists were right it would mean radioactive fallout and radiation sickness across the entire country, nuclear winds howling across a bare land, a long, dark, cold, nuclear winter and poisoned crops and animals. Law and order might vanish altogether. Nor was it likely to stop with the two fusion bombs the aliens had planned. Retaliation would surely follow from both sides, until the entire world was destroyed. I felt bleakness and horror beyond imagining.

I slept for an hour or so and woke early to a grey cool day on Saturday morning. Although there was no school, and I was exhausted, I knew there was no chance of going back to sleep, so I got up and went downstairs. I wanted to talk to Fenella. I wanted her to tell me it was all right. In the kitchen Mum smiled at me for the first time since the incident with the 'eagle'.

'Are you going to come and help me with the shopping, Dominic?'

I toyed unenthusiastically with a piece of toast. The end of the world was imminent and Mum wanted to go shopping.

'If you want me to.'

'I have a huge shop to do at Sainsbury's.'

I shrugged. There were certainly worse things in life than a huge shop at Sainsbury's, though at one time I would not have said so. I wondered if there was any point in shopping, if there was any point in doing anything at all.

Dad cleared his fishing tackle out of the boot of the car and Mum, Auntie, Julia and I set off for Taunton.

At the supermarket we had to go down to the lowest floor of the underground car park before we found parking.

'It's going to be one of those days,' said Mum.

While they started to shop I went quickly down the hill to buy myself a large, hardbacked notepad in which to write down all that had happened to me over the past few weeks.

'Huge shop' had not been an exaggeration. By the time I returned to the supermarket they had filled two trolleys. Julia and I wheeled one each from the check-out to the lifts while Mum followed behind helping Auntie and checking the shopping list to see where we needed to go next.

'Oh no,' she groaned. Two of the lifts were out of order and a long queue of people stretched away from the other three. Our car was ten floors below ground so there was no question of our carrying all the shopping down the stairs. We resigned ourselves to a long wait.

That was when the four minute warning went off.

At first no one knew what it was. It was a spine-chilling siren, the sound rising and falling, rising and falling. The crowd by the lifts frowned at each other. I went hot, then cold, and for the first time in my life felt faint. I held tightly on to the handle of the trolley, while black spots danced in front of my eyes. Julia peered at me, then was distracted by the continuing sound of the siren.

'Mum? What's that?' She looked in bewilderment at my mother. '*Mum!*' She shook Mum's arm. Then the speechless wide-eyed look on my mother's face silenced her.

'Is it the road works?' asked a very old man ahead of us. People were craning their necks towards the street, then turning to each other. The expression on my mother's face began to be repeated on others.

A lift arrived, full, and those emerging from it stood still and looked questioningly at the rest of us. No one who was waiting moved to get in and go down to their cars.

'I reckon they're testing the air-raid sirens,' said the very old man. 'They always used to, regular-like.'

The old woman with him shook her head. 'They don't do that any more, John. That was seventy years ago.'

The old man clutched their few purchases tightly in a string bag and spoke in a high adenoidal voice. 'Well I reckon the Germans are coming.'

'No no, that war's long over. The Germans are on our side now.'

'It would be the Russians again now, wouldn't it?' It was a middle-aged woman with a perm who spoke. An icy silence fell over the crowded lobby. Two teenage girls with long hair and summer dresses came out of the women's loos, and stared around them nervously. One bit her lip and giggled.

Gooseflesh was standing out on my arms and legs, although the day had become warm. I touched Mum's arm.

'Mum, we'd better leave the shopping and go and get the car. We've got to get home.'

Her awful stare of realisation turned towards me.

'I paid a hundred and ninety pounds for all this shopping.'

Gently I detached Julia's hands from the handle of the trolley.

'I know, Mum.'

'We'll need food, if this is . . .'

I thought quickly. She was right.

'Mum, why don't you and Julia go down the stairs

and get the car. I'll look after Auntie and take these trolleys round to the car park exit.'

We glanced at Auntie and I saw with shock that silent tears were rolling down her cheeks. Mum reached out and clasped her aunt's arm, then turned back to me.

'I daren't leave you both here alone.'

'It's all right, Mum. Nobody's panicking yet.'

Voices were jabbering all around us now.

'Is it the Russians?'

'Is it the bomb?'

'Oh God! My children are at home!'

Suddenly people started to run, and still the siren went on, and on.

'Go on, Mum. I'll see you by the car park exit.' I gave her and Julia a shove. Mum suddenly grabbed me by the shoulders and hugged me tightly, then she and Julia raced for the stairs, their faces ghost-white in the ill-lit lobby.

I turned back to Auntie. Her dark old eyes looked at me, red-rimmed, then she moved to take one of the trolleys from me.

'It's all right, Auntie. You can't manage one of these. They're much too heavy. Here, you hold on to the side and have your walking stick in your other hand.' I started to move, pushing one trolley and pulling the other. The siren still blared. A young man with a dark beard touched my arm.

'Stay here. We'll all be safer under cover. Any protection's better than none.'

'What is it?' the old man with the string bag asked

him, as though he ought to know. The young man with the beard turned towards him and shrugged his shoulders in their green corduroy jacket. I could see him struggling to control his own overwhelming fear.

'It's just conceivable . . . that something too awful for words has happened.'

A shudder of primitive terror ran through those of us who remained. Suddenly the place stank of sweat. Faintly in the distance a loudspeaker van became audible, its words as yet indistinguishable against the barbarous moaning of the siren.

'Thank you but I have to get out,' I said to him. 'Excuse me, I have to get out.' The trolley swivelled and swung and crashed against my ankles. I moved awkwardly and tried to get past and round people. Those who were running had gone now. Everyone else stood still. I looked around at them.

'You should all try and get home,' I said. 'There's no point in staying here. Go down the stairs and get your cars.'

Some people nodded, as though awakening from a deep sleep, and started to move. In others, the paralysis remained.

'Maybe we'd be better off in the lifts. You know, protected,' called out a young woman in a tremulous voice. She picked up her romper-clad toddler, and a few others moved with her towards the lifts.

'Don't!' shouted the man with the beard and the corduroy jacket. 'You'll be trapped in there! Sealed in! The electricity will go off.'

'Is it the bomb? Is it? Is it?' shouted a fat, red-faced

171

man with a hearing aid. People began to cry. I tried to haul the loaded trolleys behind me now, but people were tripping over them as the crowd started moving towards the stairs, full shopping bags bumping at their sides. Suddenly Auntie hung her walking stick on one of the two trolleys and seized the handle from me.

'Come on, lad. This cart will help prop me up.' She started to push and the trolley moved forward, powered by Auntie's unsteady weight. I pushed the other one and we started to make progress. Then softly Auntie began to sing.

'"Hey Jude,
Don't make it bad,
Take a sad song
And make it better . . ."'

Her voice was tuneful and she knew all the words of the old 1960s Beatles song. We gained momentum as we came out into the open and Auntie's voice soared. Behind us other voices joined in.

'"Hey Jude,
Don't be afraid . . ."'

We were walking along beside the plate-glass windows of the supermarket now and I saw that there were still people inside. Cashiers still sat at their computers. It was unbelievable. People coming out through the automatic doors stared around them, and then at the road works. Auntie's trolley had gained too much speed by now and she was tottering, so I steered it by its side towards the railings and we bumped along them until we reached the corner by the car park exit.

'All right Auntie? We'll wait here for . . .'

Suddenly the sky lightened slightly in the north. It was as though the sun had come out to brighten a cloudy day. Then the lights went off in Sainsbury's and a gentle breeze started to blow. The automatic glass exit door stopped opening and wide-eyed people began beating on the inside of the glass. Then with a dying, sighing whisper, the siren stopped.

Thirty-two

Cars were flooding out of the car park. Auntie and I stood for ten minutes watching other cars leave before Mum screeched our estate car up to ground level and out into the street. She bumped it up on to the pavement so that other cars could continue passing. She gave me and Auntie another brief, fervent hug, then the four of us began piling carrier bags and boxes of shopping into the boot. Julia was crying. Mum's eyes were cold and dry.

'It must be Bristol,' she said quietly at one point. 'Sue is in Bristol.' Sue was one of her old school friends, my godmother. The sky was becoming lighter still in the north, a strange yellow, like mustard. Mum in her blue dress and tan silk scarf looked like a figure from a mediaeval tapestry in that light. 'We must get home before the fallout reaches us,' she muttered, tossing bags in and not caring about flattened meringues and squashed tomatoes. The wind blew a little more strongly.

People were running in all directions now, and cars were driving on the wrong side of the road.

'I expect it was the docks. That would be why they hit Bristol. Where else, I wonder? London? Manchester? I wonder if we have retaliated.'

I knew we would have. One in the East and one in the West. St Petersburg and Bristol.

Mum slammed the boot shut with frenzied haste and thrust Julia and Auntie into the back of the car.

'I'd better have you in the front with me in case there's trouble,' she said softly. She raised her voice. 'Everyone strapped in? We must go quickly now. There will be complete chaos in a few minutes. I just hope we've got enough hydrogen in the tank to get us home.'

We pushed into one of the lines of traffic and moved as far as the corner round which I had pulled the trolleys. The old man with the string bag had collapsed by the automatic exit doors and was being given mouth-to-mouth resuscitation by the young woman with the toddler. A pregnant woman with a pushchair raced past us. A young boy took a loaf of bread from a trolley which stood abandoned on the pavement. His face held a glazed look of stupid terror. The traffic was slowing. It became motionless and I saw that the traffic lights were not working. Dust hung pewter grey against the yellowing bruise of a sky. Suddenly we could hear the loudspeaker van again.

'Attention! Attention!' it called. Car windows were rolled down and engines quietened their revving. 'This is Taunton Deane Borough Council. Do not panic. I repeat, do not panic. You are in no immediate danger at the moment. I repeat, you are in no immediate danger. A nuclear fusion device has fallen on Bristol. Return to your homes and close all doors and windows. Block up chimneys. Radioactive fallout is not expected to endanger life in this area. The rule of law will be maintained at all times, despite possible failures in power and communications . . .' The voice died away as the traffic in Mary Street moved again. We shifted in our queue, then stopped, shifted then stopped.

Mum reached out and turned the car radio on. A loud crackling noise made us all jump. She pressed the station buttons one by one. On one, faint military music sounded against the crackling. On another, a voice said clearly '. . . at Downing Street . . .' then was lost. Mum tried all the buttons again, then gave up and switched off.

I felt a blank helplessness. You expect to experience a whole range of new emotions when the absolute worst has just occurred. Instead I was numb, sick, reluctant to believe what I knew was true. Suddenly another voice spoke in my ear. For a moment I thought it was the loudspeaker van again, but then I realised it was a woman's voice and that it was speaking to me personally.

'Dominic? Dominic?'

I pulled my left earlobe in disbelief.

'Yes?'

Mum glanced at me, then went back to concentrating on the traffic.

'Dominic, this is BS One.'

I straightened in my seat.

'Who?'

'BS One, Dominic. The gadget maker.'

I covered my other ear to shut out the sounds of shouting, hooting and revving. The voice went on.

'Don't reply if it's too difficult, Dominic. First, I have a message from Fenella, Claude and Mitzalie. They are all right. They are far away in deep space, too far off to communicate with you. I am speaking to you on the new secret wavelength I have just set up.'

Mum was looking at me again. 'Is there something wrong with your ear, Dominic?'

I scarcely heard her. 'Oh, yes ma'am.'

Mum clicked her tongue. 'Well we'll see to it when we get home.'

The voice went on, while my skin prickled with disbelief. This was BS One, the leader, the gadget maker. 'Dominic, your friends will get in touch with you when they can. They send their love. Now, you and Peter Baxendale are the only two Black Star members left on Earth. We're going to be asking a lot from you in the coming months. The fight against the United Council of Planets and its brainwashing must go on more strongly than ever after what nearly happened to Earth. The Council . . .'

'What?' My voice came out as a strangled cry.

'I said we'll see to it when we get home,' answered Mum, turning on the windscreen wipers against the dust.

'Nearly? Nearly happened? It *has* happened . . .' I exclaimed in despair. Didn't they know anything up there?

Mum was saying something else but I did not hear

what, because the voice was stating the unbelievable in my ear.

'Oh, it was convincing was it? You really have to hand it to them. Their illusions get more impressive all the time . . .'

'What?' I was shouting now. 'What?'

'Oh shut up, Dominic!' screamed Julia from the back of the car. 'Why are you talking gibberish?' I realised I had broken into the interplanetary language in response to BS One's use of it.

'Hush hush.'

I looked behind me and saw that Auntie was patting Julia's hand. Auntie smiled at me.

'I did wonder if that monster really was a dream, lad. Seems to me you've got a bit of explaining to do.' I gaped at her, but the voice was continuing in my ear.

'It was a cruel illusion, Dominic. That was why they needed so many people down there on Earth, to set it up. Originally they did actually want to blow you all up but they couldn't because of . . .' There was a crash and a shocked gasp sounded in my ear. 'Oh God! They're coming for me! I must speak quickly. I think they're breaking down the doors . . .' I could hear a commotion in the background now. 'Dominic . . . Dominic . . .' There were thuds and shouts suddenly very close in my ear.

'BS One?'

But she interrupted me, speaking very fast suddenly. 'There will be difficult times ahead on Earth, Dominic. People are going to be very confused by this and your leaders are all still in a dangerous mental state. The

Council decided to substitute an illusion because they thought your leaders were going to set the bombs off too soon, before they could relocate the . . .'

There were other voices, faintly, and the sound of violent movements, then BS One's voice in a desperate, rapid whisper.

'Dominic, find Batworthy. He's heading south . . .'

There was an electronic screech and the line went dead.

'Oh God. Oh God.' Tears began to pour down my face. Mum reached out and clasped my hand tightly in her own for a moment, looking very worried. The traffic moved and dust blew harder against the windscreen.

I put my head back against the headrest and tried to make sense of my thoughts. What had BS One meant? Why did the United Council of Planets not dare to let us blow ourselves up yet, when they so obviously wanted to? What, or whom, was it that they needed to relocate?

I felt a brief, shocking sense of loss at the realisation of BS One's capture and of what would happen to her, and at the thought of Fenella and the others so far away beyond the stars. Then I realised with certainty that I would go out there again, somehow or other. The fight was only just beginning. I must do what BS One had asked me to, perhaps the last thing she would ever ask of anybody. I must find Mr Batworthy, and with him try and discover the real secret of the aliens' presence on Earth.

'Well?' It was Auntie speaking from the back of the car. Everyone looked at her, then at me. I glanced outside at the lines of traffic and at anxious motorists and passengers settling down for a long wait. This was a lull. It was only a lull, but in it I might have time to tell my story.

I looked at the hard-backed grey notebook in a paper bag on the floor at my feet. Tonight I would begin to write down all that had happened to me.

I looked around at my family in the car. I hesitated.

'You wouldn't think . . .' I began, and paused. How did one say this? I pulled my seatbelt a little looser and settled myself sideways in my seat. 'You wouldn't think to look at me, would you, that I was a dangerous alien . . .'

PULLING THE PLUG
ON THE UNIVERSE
Maggie Prince

The world – and the Universe – have moved on since I wrote *Memoirs of a Dangerous Alien*.

We had a few months free from alien interference here on Earth, and then they were back. This time, instead of their mind control affecting politicians, they turned my own family into terrifying strangers.

Soon I was the only functioning Black Star Gang member left on Earth. Pursued by secret agents of the United Council of Planets, I knew it was up to me to find the Council's all powerful central computer and put it out of action. It might be too late to save my family and best friend, but perhaps it was not too late to save Earth. I knew I must try . . . by pulling the plug on the Universe.

Now read on . . .

We'd better get some more information about this planet we're heading for,' I said, and activated the voice control of the computer.

'Computer, do you have any information about the planet Bench Hellezine?'

The computer gave a sniff. I stared at it in astonishment, thinking I must have misinterpreted the sound. Then it spoke. 'Just because I've been stuck in a loft for three months doesn't mean I'm totally out of touch, you know.'

Peter and I both gaped at the machine. I was about to speak but the computer clearly had not finished yet.

'I'm actually Fenella Summerling's computer, anyway, so I don't really think I have to tell you anything. Not that anyone cares what a computer feels. I'm sure I don't know what you're doing here. No one bothers to tell me anything. Fenella went off without a word of goodbye . . .' The computer's metallic voice was sounding more and more upset. 'It's so thoughtless. Fenella had programmed me in *special ways*. Nothing you would understand, of course . . .' Its voice trailed away.

'Oh dear,' Peter whispered. 'A computer that's having a nervous breakdown.' He raised his voice again. 'How do you mean, Fenella had programmed you in special ways?'

The computer was silent for a moment.

'I couldn't possibly say,' it eventually replied in a prim tone.

'We're friends of Fenella, too,' I said to it. There was another pause.

'Well, bad luck. I don't suppose she said goodbye to you either.'

'Oh dear, the poor thing's feelings are really hurt.' Peter kept his voice low, but not low enough.

'I don't need your sympathy!' There was obviously nothing wrong with the computer's hearing. 'Just don't do anything else stupid like going through roofs. And another thing, you don't seem to be aware that this gravity-blaster is fitted with one of the new invisibility screens, so I suggest you use it next time instead of making such an exhibition of yourselves. It's the button on the far left.'

I loosened my seat belt and sat forward in my seat.

'Thank you.' I glanced at the button. It did say 'invisibility screen'. This was something new. Alien technology never failed to astound me. I thought for a moment and then spoke to the computer again. 'Listen, computer, we need your co-operation. Do you have a name?'

'Nothing I intend telling you.'

Peter sighed, but I had had a sudden thought.

'Computer, my name is Dominic. Didn't we meet

once before aboard the Starship Ashkey?' These were the secret passwords of the Black Star Gang. Softly, inside the computer, something gave a faint click, then without my touching it the display screen came on. The metallic voice spoke again.

'That's different then, Dominic. Perhaps we did and perhaps we didn't. I really wouldn't like to say. Anyway, my name is Newt, and information about Bench Hellezine is appearing on our screen right now.'

I was uncertain as to whether 'our' was supposed to indicate co-operation or royal status.

'Thank you.' I leaned forward again and studied the closely packed information on the screen. It was interspersed with maps, diagrams and low level aerial photographs. Bench Hellezine appeared to be a bleak place. It was a small planet about the size of Earth's moon, but pear-shaped and plagued by volcanoes and earthquakes. Its equatorial regions were barren and hot, its polar regions barren and cold. Its people were poor and lived on Council aid because more often than not their crops failed as a result of the harsh climate.

Newt spoke again just as Peter and I scrolled on to the last screenful of information.

'I'm taking us out of hypervortex. Bench Hellezine is visible on your control screen and will be visible through the dome in five minutes. Solar flares can be seen on Bench Hellezine's sun, worth looking at if you like fireworks. Look out through the right side of the dome to see them. I find that my function is being affected by them.' I looked at the computer in alarm, then out through the right side of the glass dome over our heads. For a moment I couldn't speak. The sight was awesome.

Bench Hellezine's sun was an orange and blue star. Great columns of purple flame stood out all around it. The words that Peter spoke then, in a hushed voice, are not permitted by my publishers to be repeated here.

When Newt spoke again, his tones were distorted. I refer to it as him, which is ridiculous, I know, since it is a machine and not a person, but given the personality with which Fenella had programmed it, it was difficult to remember this.

For anyone who is wondering why I refer to it as him rather than her, there are two reasons. One is that the tones and cadences of its voice were masculine, and the other is because it sounded as if it were in love with Fenella.

'Two minutes to touchdown,' Newt informed us in these distorted tones. 'There are incapacitators in the cupboards at the back if you want them.'

I reached behind me and slid back a door of the small storage cupboard. It seemed a long time since I had seen one of these gun-shaped instruments which could temporarily paralyse or knock out an enemy. I took out both of them, complete with holsters, and handed one to Peter. I also took out a pair of solar powered binoculars.

The planet was clearly visible outside the dome now. It was indeed pear-shaped. It looked like a chunk of rock untidily hewn from the side of some mountain. Newt spoke again, with even worse dislocation in his voice.

'Dominic . . . Nodimic . . . it may be . . .' The voice died away on a hollow whine. Thoroughly alarmed now, I stabbed at the enhancer button. The voice came back in a ghostly bass croak. 'I hope you can fly this crate on manual, Micinod, because this force field is leaving me a little high. I must warn you . . . it may be . . . it may be that the other computers on this planet are similarly affected . . .' The voice sank and faded further. I pressed the enhancer button again. Peter had taken over flying the gravity-blaster on manual. A series of clicks came from within the computer.

The hollow booming whisper was almost impossible to decipher now, but what it sounded like was, 'The people of Bench Hellezine may not be correctly brain-processed, Mickey Mouse. They may be over-processed or not processed at all. Beware of them, Nickynoc, beware . . . they may be misprocessed to the point of mania . . .' Then Newt was silent.

A few moments later, we landed for the first time on an alien planet.

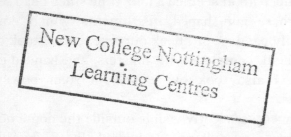